MW01147091

NEEDLE ASH

A TALE OF THE ETERNAL DREAM

BOOK 1:
KNIVES OF DARKNESS

BY
DAVID VAN DYKE STEWART

WITH
ILLUSTRATIONS BY BRAD LYNN

Contents

AUTHOR'S NOTES

Needle Ash is a new story that I've written in a universe that is not new. I published another book called *The Water of Awakening* that is set in the same world, but in a different geographic location with a different protagonist and written in a different style altogether. There are several characters that make appearances in both stories, though you won't meet them in this volume. While *Needle Ash* is technically a sequel to *Water of Awakening,* reading that previous book is not at all required to understand this story, though you may find value in it, for it provides a great amount of exploration into the nature of the world and the magic within it.

Within this volume (and the subsequent ones) you will find art plates by Brad Lynn. One of the things I will point out is the accuracy of the arms and armor he depicts, which is one of the reasons I wanted to work with him (I actually found him through a HEMA group, a mutual interest of ours). You can find more of his work at https://www.facebook.com/BradLynnDrawings

The Central
DIVINE STRAND
In The Fourth Dominion

Orcish
Dry Lands

Brown Mountains

Artalland

Travertine
Hinterlands

Crafter's Mountains

Toll River

Havara

Forgoroto

Toll Bay

Landera

Villaros River

Calasora

Pious's Fall

Ferralla

Red River

Structania

Datala Sea

Bant

Balta

DVS
✳ '17

Needle Ash

Book I:
Knives of Darkness

I: On the Battlefield

The sweets of life are enjoyed seldom and by few;
But the bitterness of death is tasted by all, and
There you find bitterness is another relative thing
Among many other relative, mutable things
That make a mundane world you call immutable

But for the honorable, there is no death;
Only a return to the dream.

Dreams to a living man are like gazing through a clouded mirror,
whereas the dreams of death are like crystal water
Only beyond the hazy veil of the mundane, the old dreams, shall we
meet face to face and see each other as we truly are.

-The Apocrypha of Verbus, fourth proclamation.

This is a bad day to give to battle, Michael thought. He walked through the muddy tracks of the forward camp, grumbling as he felt mud slip between his sabatons and his boots. Water was dripping through a gap in his open visor, running along his nose into his beard, making his helm seem stifling even in the cold rain. He flexed his hands, willing the nerves that fought against death before each battle to obey his mind. As he ambled through the wagons and tents, he saw Angelico, his favorite lieutenant, huddling under a makeshift canvas canopy held up by barrels of unopened brandy. These were pieces reserved for a celebration, the occurrence of which seemed to Michael to be less likely with each passing day and each stalemated skirmish with the Ferrallese army.

"Ho, highness," Angelico said from where he sat, bowing his head and thumping his bare fist to his breastplate. "I would stand to salute you, sir, but I'm afraid without my squire to assist in the effort I would knock over this lovely shelter."

Michael chuckled and stopped. "We wouldn't want that. We'd risk spilling the king's vittles."

"No need to upset the old man so far from the comforts of home. I'll stay seated." Angelico picked up a bowl of steamy stew sitting on a nearby barrel. He tore something up and dropped it in, and then shoveled some of the grey, thick food into his mouth. "As for my own comforts, I am thankful. The palate be a fickle thing, sir."

"Certainly for a man from the wine country. By the end of this campaign, I think those dried peppers will be worth their weight in gold."

"They already are to me," Angelico said. "But I have some saved for you, in the eventuality that the stocks reserved for the royal family begin to dwindle." He took a sip and nodded. "Where are you heading already suited up?"

"Officers' meeting. We'll be going over the battle plans."

"Already? Are they that close?"

"Just on the other side of the foothills, our scouts report."

"I'm not invited to this meeting?"

"Top brass only, I'm afraid," Michael said. "I expect you'll be serving with me again, waiting for the inevitable call to guard the retreat after we stalemate."

"Don't let your father hear you talking like that."

"I won't. Don't worry. Believe me, there's nothing I'd rather do than take our cavalry into a real assault…" Michael shrugged. "I am not the commander."

"Good luck to us, and hold your tongue, my lord," Angelico said.

"I will, my friend. When your squire overcomes his laziness, make sure your company knows that the battle is likely to be fought today. I want inspections done before we have to give the order to move, understand?"

"Yes sir."

"And make sure they eat hearty. And make sure the priests give them the goddess's blessing if they desire."

Angelico slammed his fist to his chest again as Michael walked on. The dreary rain seemed to have dampened most spirits much more than Angelico's, but the prince, upon hearing the news of the battle council, had felt the churning anxiety of war in his stomach; the lurching and dread, and even excitement, left little room for feeling melancholy.

He arrived at the command tent at the same time as his brother Johan, who wore a cloak over his armor and head. He gave him a frowning nod as they paused in front of the flap.

"How is your legion?" Johan said in his calm, even voice.

Michael thumped his chest in salute. "Ready and willing. This is a battle council, correct? Why no lower officers?"

"The king has his reasons, I suspect."

"Which he will not voice to us."

"Be patient and more thoughtful. Such is the prerogative of his position."

"After you," Michael said, lifting the flap of the tent. As he followed his brother in, he removed his helm and shook the water off of it.

Inside, their father, King Eduardo the Black, was leaning over a large table with a newly drawn map. His hair, long since yielded from black to mottled grey, hung damp on his gilded and embossed armor. Behind him stood the wide girth of General Butler Dolanari, the battlefield commander, and Towler, the high mage of the first army.

"The princes are here, your highness," said Towler. An elfish blonde man from the north of indeterminable age, he leaned on his staff as if crippled, his blue eyes trembling as he took in the princes. Michael shuddered slightly under the gaze.

"Good. Good," said the King, his eyes still gazing over the lines of the map. Michael stepped nearer and saw that it depicted in detail the elevated expanse to the west of their camp, where they expected to meet the forces of Ferralla in the first open battle in months. There was a tension in the room, acrid in the silence filled only with the sound of rain softly falling on the tent. Butler, a sweaty man in the normal heat of Artalland, seemed to be dripping like a cold pot. Michael wiped his own wet brow.

Everyone in the tent knew, succeed or fail, this battle would be the end of the campaign. Supplies were lower than spirits, and already the army had been out in the field longer than was standard.

They could return home as heroes, forcing an armistice or at least a regrouping of the enemy, or they would all be scrambling against an invasion in earnest. Conquest, the intent of the original campaign, had been all but given up on.

At last, the king spoke. "General Butler and I have devised a battle plan. This has been well-considered for some time. Even the location of this camp." The king cast a dark eye backward to the general.

The general cleared his throat, wiping sweat from his large pate as he did so. He produced from a small box on the table a series of wooden blocks, colored to indicate the various companies. He placed them on the map carefully as he spoke.

"The battle plain we have selected is beyond the hills to our west," he said in his characteristic gravelly drawl. "It gives us some distinct advantages." He approached the war table and pointed to some shallow topography lines. "We'll have the high ground here and here, useful for both observation by command and as a bulwark should the tide turn against us."

"What about those other hills?" Michael said, pointing to a series of lines further west. "Seems like that would give Ballaco and his army some of the same advantages."

"Listen to the entire plan before asking foolish questions, Michael," the king said darkly, lifting his chin as if to look down on his son, who was taller than he was.

Michael bowed his head and touched his fist to his chest as he stepped backward, hoping his father did not see him blush.

Butler cleared his throat again. "Yes, as I was saying. We have decided on this battlefield. Ballaco will give battle to us here because he sees the same advantages as the prince. It's a good neutral battle plain. Or so he will think. He will also see our encampment as being dangerously close to the field proper, and press aggressively to force a rout in the middle."

"Which we will give him, I'm sure," the king said.

Butler nodded. "We're banking on him disregarding this ravine to the north here, as it will be impassable for cavalry moving in wider formations than pairs. We plan on putting two companies of infantry into play there, along with one cavalry platoon and a detachment of dragoons. In these riparian woods they won't be seen by the casual lookout, and Ballaco will expect our flanking maneuvers to come from our light and heavy cavalry, not infantry."

Michael wanted to speak up, to counter-indicate the general. Flanking with infantry, especially that far afield, was a tactic doomed to fail. The Ferralla legions would form a shield wall on their flank before two companies of infantry could mount the hills and cover the distance to the battle plain. Even before he could open his mouth to speak, he noticed his brother gazing at him with a look that approached contempt, and so Michael remained silent.

As if also sensing this tension, Butler chuckled and pointed to a point further west on the map. "The goal of this other pair of companies is not to flank the enemy directly, but to engage their reserves, which I expect to be stationed here, with their own forward camp further west by this creek, here. With the reserves occupied, there will be no reinforcement of their forward push.

"Our plan, thus, is this: We will engage in a standard set of tactics after the standard failure of entreatment. Our cavalry, which is superior in number and in strength, ought to be able to intercept theirs and have room to harry the flanks of their forward infantry, as well as press on their archer companies once the fighting begins. Their mage corps will likely be operating as one unit, thinking to counter our own, which they have been successful with so far, though they shall not be this time."

"You have other plans?" Towler said in his deep and thin, almost brittle voice.

Butler nodded. "Mages will be dispersed into the companies, with priority given to cavalry, of course. In that position they cannot be counterspelled efficiently, and will be a destructive asset to those companies. That will leave the rest of our men more open to their mages, but we can endure it, and they will suffer greater losses spread across the lines. Michael will be in charge of the northern cavalry companies. Johan, you will take charge of your legion as well as the southern cavalry company normally attached to the second legion, due to the practical limitation of commanding across the battlefield."

"What about the rest of my legion?" Michael said. "I'm just to command the cavalry?"

"Your infantry and archer company will be in the critical position of reserve," Butler said. "Which I was about to say."

"Critical position?" Michael said, raising his voice. He stepped forward, feeling sweat burst anew on his face. "How is waiting for the battle to go sour a critical position?"

"Silence," King Eduardo said firmly, holding up his hand to Michael

For a moment, Michael was silent, but it only gave him time to feel his anger more thoroughly. "We've always had our own reserves for each legion, father. Why do my men have to stand on the sidelines? They will be ashamed to wait out the last battle."

"Isn't it enough that *you* aren't sitting it out?" Eduardo said, straightening up. "Your quest for glory is in no danger, leading your cavalry."

"This isn't about glory!"

"Silence!" Eduardo's face grew taught. "Or I will relieve you and hire a new high captain. He may be of lesser blood but brighter mind, and thus more worthy of my grace."

Michael wanted nothing more at that moment than to shout down at his father, make plain his favoritism and foolishness, but the threat contained him. He was not the crown prince. He needed to have a military command to have a future in the court, and his father knew it. A sickening feeling in his stomach told Michael his father would likely always lord it over him.

"Forgive me," Michael said.

"Forgiveness is earned through diligence and penance," the king replied, his eyes turning back to the map. "May the gods speak true."

Butler cleared his throat again. "Yes. Well, our light cavalry will perform its normal role, engaging weak points and withdrawing, as well as disrupting the enemy charges. Heavy cavalry will wait for my command to hit the infantry lines. Michael, your dragoons will need to be working their way across the northern lines, which will inevitably form in response to our cavalry. This will stretch out the greater part of their fighting force.

"Our primary goal is to stretch out their infantry, making it harder to contain our mages. Johan, make sure your lieutenants know that they may fold their lines backward. A slow retreat East is what we wish to create, keeping as many of our men on their feet and healthy as possible. As our lines fold back, I expect Ballaco, or his officers, to push for the rout." Butler pushed a few thin blocks of wood forward, and Michael could see his intent. The enemy legion's infantry, rather than maintaining the great maniples necessary to hold a shield wall, would essentially have formed a large hollow ring surrounding the Artalland army.

"Your reserves, Michael, will relieve the first legion's front lines and prevent the rout. Once they stall out, we will use our archers to attack the middle of the field. A few good volleys, and then I will lead the king's elite heavy cavalry, supplemented by heavy horse from each of your legions, to punch through the lines here. We'll push west and crush their reinforcements and put the whole west end of the field into a rout, which the light cavalry will then ride down. After that it's just a matter of cleanup, taking prisoners, and accepting Ballaco's sword."

"You are sure it will work like this?" Johan said.

Butler nodded. "I've spent the last few months getting to know Ballaco the way only a general can know a fellow warrior. He's as thirsty for a victory as we are. The morale of his army is likely as bad as our own. He wants a rout in the front lines, to give his men the courage to push for victory. He will not think twice about pressing an advantage he thinks we have overlooked."

"What of our own morale?" Johan said.

"Discipline will act in place of confidence," the king said. "As long as each of you has maintained it in your men."

"We have, sir," Michael and Johan said together.

*

Michael paused beside the eternally grim-faced Gadero, his sergeant major, on the hill and looked out over the battle plain. Calot, as he called his destrier, was anxious and padded the ground beside Gadero's lighter horse, which was placid, almost sad. The rain was lighter now, a mere sprinkle, and though the sky was leaden he could see clearly the main infantries of the Artallan and Ferrallese armies as they played their lines in the mud. He watched a shield wall fold in the Ferralla line, watched as Johan's infantry pushed into the gap, only to fall back as they were surrounded by the rear lines.

The battle, oddly, was going too well for his side. The Ferrallese were not pushing hard enough, and though their infantry had proved subtly superior in previous engagements, it was not advancing as planned, but instead pulling a series of formation maneuvers that left the center of the field empty but made their shield wall stronger against the light cavalry and dragoons that harried the north and south sides of the field. The Ferrallese cavalry had proved inadequate, and Michael's knights had found little sport in the chase of the Ferrallese knights back to the archery lines.

The best Michael could guess was that General Ballaco, favored commander of Queen Alanrae (who Michael recalled was rumored to be a mage), was betting heavily on his mage corps, formed of a small line of mounted units in light armor, to do the work their light cavalry could not. There were some ten staffmen that Michael could see through his spyglass, more than half of them possessing the light frames and height of women. Ten was a serious force, even if most of them seemed by display of skill to be novices rather than adepts. The unit of mages moved about between the infantry formations, attempting to lob fire, upend the earth, or otherwise confuse and disorient the Artallan infantry. It was working, but not well enough to push the Ferrallese army into a solid advance as Butler had predicted. Somehow, watching them work made Michael uneasy, giving him a feeling that he was forgetting something important.

"What think you, highness?" Gadero said, watching Michael. His dark face, weathered in a way that diminished his minor battle scars, was relaxed as he gazed westward. Michael handed him the spyglass and removed his helmet, letting the light rain cool his face.

"Mayhap we won't need to do any fancy strategizing," the old soldier said, focusing on one of his closer infantry units, which was holding its own against a solid shield wall and harassment from a group of enemy horse archers. "I reckon we could just hammer these fools home anyhow."

"I'm concerned with their mage company."

"If that's what you want to call it. They're not doing much."

"That's what concerns me. In the last skirmish, they were devastating. It took Towler and two more senior mages to counter them effectively, and it was exhausting for them. They're holding back, maybe trying to save their energy or focus - whatever it is for mages - for something else."

Gadero put down the spyglass and nodded. "They could be waiting for our reserves. Or they may have a few of theirs kept back."

"That's what I was thinking, but…" Michael grunted. "I have an uneasy feeling."

"Ain't no easy feeling on the battlefield, sire. Thirty years and I still feel the sickness in every swing."

"It's something other than that, Sergeant. But you're right, it's probably nothing."

"Begging your pardon, my prince, but that is not what I said. I never said it was nothing. I said there ain't no easy feeling on the battlefield."

"Johan might prove otherwise."

Gadero grunted softly, then said, "I've lived through some hells, sire. Those gut feelings sent me to plenty of places that made me live. I don't feel it today though, sire."

Michael nodded. "Well, we shall have to see what happens. Have the second dragoons and third heavy cavalry move to that empty spot over there. That maniple is misshaping their shield wall. I think we could punch through and do some damage if they won't do what we want. Then have them fall back. The Ferrallese will have to reform closer to our objectives and our other maniple there. We may yet get this plan on foot."

"I'll delay that order for a moment, sire. Here comes young Palsay."

Michael saw the young man riding full steam from a break in the light wood, his horse foaming at the mouth. He was bleeding from scratches on his unhelmed face and streaked with dirt. He reined in as he pulled up.

"Michael! Uh, Captain... your highness, sir!" he stammered as his horse tossed its head.

"Enough with the titles, get on telling us how you lost your helmet, soldier," Gadero said. "And where you got a horse."

The young man wiped his face and took a breath. "Yeah. Sir! I've just been over the Northern rise, sir. Scouting, sir, my orders, sir. My helmet fell off. This was a dragoon's horse, sir. I hated to take it, but, sir-"

"Come off and just tell us, man!" Michael said, seeing the shock in Palsay's eyes.

Palsay nodded. "The Farallese have assembled and are marching down the northern ravine."

"How many?" Michael said.

"I would say… Fifteen-hundred men. Most of their reserves."

"Shit," Gadero said, then looked to Michael. "Pardon, sire."

"They aim to flank us, sire," Palsay said.

"They won't be flanking anything out there," Gadero said. "They'll come out miles north and east of the army."

Michael shook his head. "They're looking to press our forward camp, where the rest of the legion is waiting in reserve, along with a good deal of our supplies, or what's left of them. And our entrenchments are weak on the northern side."

"What about *our* companies?" Gadero said. "Our men were supposed to be running that ravine to harry the back fold of their army."

"Don't know, sir," Palsay said. "Like I said, I just saw them assembling and heading out. You think our two companies can stop them?"

"No," Michael said.

"Even with Angelico leading them?" Gadero said.

Michael shook his head. "It's a numbers game. Angelico is good, but not that good. What types of units were assembled?"

"All sorts. Cavalry and heavy infantry. A group of old-looking men and women," Palsay said.

"Women? Must be Sorcerers," Gadero said.

Palsay shrugged.

"Relay that information to Butler and the king," Michael said. "Get a fresh horse on the way if you can, on my orders. Go!"

Palsay whipped the horse with the reins and sped off.

Turning to Gadero, Michael put his helm back on. "Scratch my last orders, sergeant. I want that cavalry unit and the dragoons to meet me over yonder, near the wood."

"Sir?" Gadero said, raising an eyebrow. "What about the general's plan?"

"No wise man follows a plan beyond hope of victory. Besides, those are our men out there, and I'll be damned if I let them die without reason or hope of salvation."

"Fine," Gadero said. "But let me lead the sortie, sire. Your place on the battlefield is in command."

"Not today, sergeant. You aren't a cavalry officer. I am. If I know how to do anything, it is lead a mounted force."

"That ravine is too narrow for cavalry maneuvers, or so you said, sire."

"If the enemy is bringing horse, we can too. And that's our strength, Gadero. Always play to your strengths. You know the infantry better than any man on this battlefield, myself included. You're in charge while I run this sortie, understand?"

"Understood, sir. Give the bastards my best. And by that I mean crush a few skulls."

"As you wish!" Michael said as he bounded down the hill. In his ears he could already hear the harsh voice of Gadero gathering messengers and relaying orders.

The wind dried his face, and he felt a rush of fear and excitement. *Hold on but a little while, Angelico,* he thought to himself. *Just a while, and I know we can hold victory together!*

Michael's lance, held upright by a brass fitting on the rear of his saddle, knocked against the tree limbs of the drooping oaks. The knights surrounding him, as well as the light cavalry behind him, suffered the same annoyance, and his force, pushing through the wood at a trot, sounded like a massive wave of rolling thunder.

Michael pulled to the side to let a few men go past, then fell back in line, wanting to get a better view of his dragoons, off to the left with their shorter, lighter lances.

13

DAVID VAN DYKE STEWART

"Maybe they'll confuse this ridiculous racket with thunder," said a light airy voice to his right. "Or think it's magic. Either way, I doubt the prince considered it."

Michael lifted his visor and locked eyes with a young round-faced woman, holding a staff and armored in light mail and a helm that was slightly too large for her.

"Oh, your highness," said the woman, giving a hasty salute with her free, left hand. "I mistook you for someone else."

"Obviously. What's your name, mage?"

"Sharona," she said, bowing her head slightly. "I was called up from the Calasora corps last month. Sorry for not knowing your armor, sire."

"I had it built for function, not so I could be easily identified as commander of an Artallan legion. Tell me, Sharona, how are you?"

The woman sighed and scratched at the padding under her helm. "I'm well enough, considering I'm in a battle, haven't had a bath in three weeks, and am likely riding to my doom." She gave him a closed-mouth smile. "I *am* talking to a prince, so that's a positive point."

"I mean, how are you with magic?"

The woman cocked her head. "Magic?"

"That's your purpose here, is it not?"

"Well, yes, but I've never had anyone just ask me. It's more like, 'You're doing that wrong.' 'This isn't like lighting a fire, you know.' 'That's too much!' 'How did you manage to get in here?' That sort of thing."

"So your sergeant was surprised you made it into training?" Michael said with a sigh.

"No, he was surprised I got into his office without unlocking it."

"Sir."

"I'm a woman."

"You are to address me as 'sir.' And you salute with your right hand. Grim's bones, didn't they teach you anything about military discipline in basic?"

"Not really, no," Sharona said. "I was called up only a week in, and I tend to forget things like that rather easily. Sorry. Sir. Sire."

"Forget it," Michael said.

"Yes, I do that."

"I see." Michael grumbled in exasperation, then took another breath and said slowly, "How are your *skills* with *magic?*"

Sharona looked away and sighed. "Um… pretty good, I suppose. I know a fair number of offensive spells. I can crack a man's femur bone using a chicken bone and a type of linking enchantment. That's quite interesting to watch."

"Excellent." Michael thought for a moment. "You thought to bring some chicken bones, yes?"

"Um, no. Sir."

"Well, we're going up against Ferralla's senior mages. Can you do anything to mitigate the threat of magic?"

"Oh, lots. But the best thing to do with mages is just kill them, I think."

"I'll keep that in mind," Michael said flatly. He spurred his horse forward to the front of the column.

Within a mile, the canopy of trees opened up and lifted a little. The river that cut through the ravine slowed and the trees thinned out, replaced by wet grasses on which the soldiers could move with much greater speed. The annoying knocking of spears on tree limbs also stopped. Soon, Michael could hear, however faintly, shouts from up ahead.

Angelico leapt free of his horse, which collapsed, full of arrows and half burned.

"To the south! To the south!" he shouted. "Get to high ground and away from that river!"

It was no use, amid the sounds of clashing shields and magic pushing through the ranks, nobody could hear his orders. Two infantry platoons were desperately trying to form up a shieldwall and maniple, but without clear command were leaving a massive gap between them.

Angelico ran for them, feeling pain in his left leg where a poleax had hit him, crushing in part of his cuisse.

"No! No! Fall back!" he shouted.

Into the gap ran five or six heavily armored Ferrallese knights bearing long-bladed lances. They had the flank of the infantry unit quickly and jabbed into the gaps of the poorly arrayed shields. Several men went down. Angelico reached the gap and ducked under a lance strike. On the ground he found a broken spear and dove for it, rolling just past another strike from a lance. He quickly tossed the broken spear at the horse in front of him. It cut along its flank below its armor, and the beast whinnied in pain.

Angelico rushed forward and grabbed at the stirrup of the rider. With a great heave, the saddle slid over the rain-slick barding and the knight toppled, striking Angelico on the breast with a warhammer even as he fell. The shield wall formed around him as Angelico drew his dagger from his belt and slammed it down onto the knight's gorget, where it stuck in the overlapping plates. The warhammer was pummeling Angelico's left side, but he barely felt the blows.

Angelico slammed his fist onto the wide, flat pommel of his dagger, driving it into the enemy's neck. He did not have time to consider the kill, for even then he felt a lance strike his left pauldron and slide, scraping along the back of his breastplate, knocking him forward and into the mud.

He felt a hand pulling at his torn cape.

"You alright Lieutenant?" It was Doboro, an infantry sergeant and (he remembered with sudden clarity) a mean card player.

"I'll live," Angelico said as he staggered to his feet.

"I don't know if I'd go that far." Doboro pointed at the enemy infantry lines, forming up under the trees. The heavy cavalry was retreating, and they heard the unmistakable sound of dozens of bows being loosed.

"Shields up!" Doboro shouted. He pulled the lieutenant toward him, into the small shelter of his great scutum, which he held aloft. Several arrows struck the reinforced wood.

After the sound dissipated, Angelico heard something else: the unmistakable sound of a cavalry charge.

"They're behind us!" Angelico shouted, looking back along the wide river plain between the woody shoulders of the ravine. He drew his sword.

"How did they do it?" Doboro said, then shouted. "Rear attack! Form up!"

Angelico laughed aloud and nearly dropped his blade as he saw a banner of a pot on a field of blue waving among two throngs of horsemen, one on each side of the river.

II: The Means of Victory

Michael rode to Angelico, relief flooding him as his friend, dirty and mud-caked, opened his visor to smile. Michael opened his in return.

"What are you doing here, sir?" Angelico said as Michael reined in Calot beside him.

"Coming to the real battle. How are losses?"

"Not so bad so far," Angelico said. "Or should I say, they could be worse. They didn't catch us totally unawares. Our squad mage sensed some magic upstream, as it were. But sir, those dragoons aren't going to do much on that side of the river."

"Just wait, my friend," Michael said.

With the arrival of the Michael's cavalry, morale in Angelico's detachment turned quickly. The infantry was able to form proper lines and advance toward the enemy. The light cavalry units intercepted the Ferrallese knights and disrupted three charges, allowing some Artallan infantry armed with crow's beaks to pull two of them down and dispatch them. With each break the Artallan cavalry would gallop back to the defensive lines, pulling in a hasty Ferrallese knight to the front, where his horse would be cut down or otherwise injured.

The dragoons, stationed on the other side of the river, dismounted and planted their oversized scutums in the dirt, where they were able to fire crossbows from cover, disrupting the enemy infantry. The Ferrallese were now having to defend on two sides.

Before the two lines could meet in earnest, an enemy mage squad, composed of clearly older men and women, most of them well-greyed, moved out with a group of knights and began casting spells at the Artallan front lines. Fire rippled over shields and over plates, scalding men as their armor continued to burn through their jacks even after the magic subsided. The earth exploded, sending men flying. Confusion set in as men went inexplicably blind.

Angelico was desperately trying to command the disheveled heavy infantrymen, but it was difficult amid the chaos. The dragoons focused on the mages, but their bolts were burning in air before the cadre of experienced staffmen.

Michael formed up the heavy cavalry for a charge, intending to disrupt the magic attack when, with a shocking suddenness, the magic ceased. Michael saw that a tall pine had fallen where the cadre had been a moment before. Two more trees were leaning and on their way to the earth, and he could see that at least one horse and rider had been caught by the first one. The mages scattered as these fell, and one more of their number was caught beneath a tree trunk. Trees continued to fall all around the enemy lines.

Michael looked to his right to see, dismounted and standing under an oak tree, Sharona, who looked like she was playing with a line of sticks stuck into the mud. She was kneeling down, eyes glassy. As she pushed one over, Michael saw another tree begin to totter.

"I'll give you a damn commendation if you keep that up!" Michael shouted to Sharona, but she seemed not to notice.

Angelico was already ordering a charge, looking to take advantage of the chaos of the falling trees. Several infantry squads, armed with smaller round shields on their backs and great long spears, moved around the wall of scutums.

"I'll bring my squads around the flank!" Michael shouted. Angelico caught his eye and nodded.

Michael led his mixed cavalry under a low canopy oak and over a soft, turf-covered hill. Arrows flew toward them at random, which Michael knew from experience to be an indicator of a strategic breakdown of the enemy. He urged Calot onward, kicking up mud and water. The horses behind him were equally unsure of their footing, but the command of the Artallan knights of their beasts was superb, and the force crested the hill and flew down the embankment into the enemy lines, which had utterly failed to either turtle with their shield wall or bear pikes properly to stop the flanking charge. Screams filled Michael's rushing ears as lances pierced armor and men fell underfoot around him.

"Second squad, pursue their mages!" he shouted. He didn't turn to see if the light cavalry obeyed him, but he knew they would. He turned his attention to the men under Calot's hooves, banging against the horse's armor. He thrust his lance downward, once, twice… on the third stab, he caught a man and Calot's massive bulk and forward momentum made him drop the lance, lest he test the oak shaft against his arm. He drew his longsword and began hacking downward. The knights on either side of him were doing the same, most of their lances broken on the enemy.

A quick glance to his left let him know the tactic had succeeded. The Ferrallese infantry was in a panic and the rear lines were no longer trying to prevent a rout from the front. Michael looked across the river to the dragoons, who were already remounting to head up-river, preventing escape across the water and moving to harass any attempt to reform after the rout.

"Knights!" Michael shouted. "Withdraw and move upfield!"

Pulling away from the mass of infantry, Michael could see through the trees a retreating mass of horsemen, including several armed with staves and short sticks, who he assumed to be mages. His second squad was actively brawling with the enemy cavalry, obscuring the mages' view and ability to put their destructive magic to work without harming their allies. Trees were falling down once again, the source of which Michael now understood, though he could not see Sharona.

"Press them! Push them up against the water!" Michael shouted. He stood up in the saddle to see the edge of the melee, and sighted, just past the enemy mages (who were now casting what spells they could beyond the throng, feebly lighting the wet grass on fire for seconds at a time) a face he had met thrice on the battlefield (including that morning) as part of the customary parlay: Ballaco D'Ash, the high general of the Ferrallese army, far from the field proper.

Michael slowed Calot and let his men gallop around him. He sheathed his sword and found hanging from his tack his compact crossbow, which he spanned with a crank and loaded with a poison-tipped bolt. He moved forward toward the melee again, then worked his way through a grove of pines. Sighting the general, he took aim, resting his arm against a nearby oak and steadying himself against the nervous twitching of his horse. He watched and waited for the general to turn and present a wide target.

Ballaco turned, but before Michael could pull the trigger he felt in his hip the unmistakable impact of an arrow and the bite that followed. Feeling the pain distantly, he fired the bolt, just as Ballaco saw him. The general put an arm up over his face, and Michael watched the bolt strike and pierce his vambrace.

They locked eyes with each other for a moment, then the general turned his horse about and called a retreat, his arm hanging limp.

Michael looked down and saw a long war arrow sticking through the mail in the gap between his cuirass and his skirted cuisses. He broke the arrow off, knowing that removing the barbed arrowhead would be impossible at that point even with a shallow wound, and turned back to join his men.

The enemy was in full retreat, but Michael knew pursuit could be dangerous; he could already see the careful lines of Angelico's infantrymen breaking apart to give chase. The dragoons on the other side of the river, well-disciplined, were already stowing their gear, the commander mounted and looking across the water for orders.

"Hold!" Michael shouted. "Bloody hold your ground!"

It was no use; Angelico's company, so close to death, now had the bloodlust upon them. Reluctantly, Michael drew his warhammer and ordered his knights into formation on the southern slope, hoping to pick up the pieces when the retreat turned on them.

The Ferrallese cavalry was moving to intercept and prevent the flanking maneuver, buying time for Ballaco and the rest of the battalion to escape. Michael engaged along with his men, hammering the enemy knights and trying to hook their armor, hoping to unhorse at least a man or two. The enemy called another retreat and galloped away, only one man down.

Within a few minutes the fatigue of the chase had worn the men down, and at last Angelico (horsed once again, but how Michael did not know) was able to rank up and order the infantry. Panting, he caught the eye of Michael, who observed the retreat from beneath an oak tree, his visor up and sweating even in the cool, damp air.

"What now, sir?" Angelico said, trying to steady the unfamiliar horse.

"We beat it back to the camp," Michael said. "Your company has seen enough of fighting for the afternoon. We need to call up the reserves and push the rout on the main field, since our initial plan has gone pear-shaped."

"What about Ballaco?"

"He'll be dead within the hour. I hit him in the arm with a poisoned bolt."

Angelico chuckled. "What a day, sire! They'll make songs about this."

"Just glad you're alive, my friend," Michael said and clapped him on the shoulder.

Michael returned to the field with his dragoons and knights to find the battle moving steadily against the Ferrallese. The Artallan reserves were called up, late by Michael's judgment, and the exhausted enemy was not able to match force. The enemy infantry was quickly scattered, and victory against the now weakened opponent was imminent. A Ferrallese messenger was brought to field with a white flag.

Michael hastened from Gadero, who had ordered the legion masterfully in his absence, wreaking apparent havoc on the enemy, toward the center field to meet with his father, brother, and General Butler.

He reined in his horse to find his father and Butler glaring at him darkly.

"What are you doing here?" the king said, hunched on his own horse, looking oddly deflated and small in his gilded armor.

"Here to take part in the surrender of the general's sword," said Michael, thinking that the formality of the surrender would be an opportunity for his father to find out he had slain the great Ballaco D'Ash.

"You'll take no such part," the king said. "Victory is for proper soldiers. Head back to the forward camp and await me there."

"What?" Michael said. "I don't understand."

"Your orders were to follow the battle plan, not divert our personnel and resources to your own objectives."

"But father," Michael said.

"Your Highness," the king growled.

Calot, as if sensing Michael's fury, began to pace underneath him as he shouted. "We defeated an entire battalion in the ravine, a full half of a legion that was making an end run to our reserves and our back. I *won* this battle for you. Without my actions-"

"Get out of my sight."

"And I killed Ballaco! This victory is mine!"

"Begone, or I'll have you hanged!"

Stunned, Michael looked to Johan, who had just arrived. "Do not make me enforce the king's will," Johan said, his face iron. He placed a hand on his sword.

Furious, Michael spurred Calot and galloped away.

*

Michael sat in the canvas chair, ignoring the discomfort of his armor as he leaned over, his elbows on his knees. The rain had ceased temporarily and he watched the west light from the flaps of the tents ignite motes of dust. They danced hypnotically before his eyes, a swirling chaos that revealed the immutable order of an air current. He realized, as he sat there in the command tent, dark except for those motes, that he had not tended to the arrow in his hip. It hurt, but not enough to make him think he had suffered much more than a scratch, though he could still feel the arrowhead stuck in his jack when he moved.

He had been given hours to tend to the wound, but he would not - at least until after he had stood before his father. Stood *up* to his father. He would stand before the king in his full armor, a knight and high captain of a legion. The empty, dark tent had been an intentional gesture, he knew, when he was called here from the forward camp of his legion.

The reverie in the camp over the past hour was almost enough to make him forget the acid of his father (and his brother, as he thought about him, was part of it too, refusing to side with him as always). Kegs of ale had been opened and flagons passed; a turkey was slaughtered and roasting. The camp followers had come in, which meant many things that did not concern the gentry, but it meant more cheer for the enlisted men, and that made the officers turn their eyes away. The only people that would miss that cheer were those in his legion assigned to guard and disarm the prisoners, of which there were many.

What had made Michael really forget about missing the surrender, however, was the cheering that the men had done for *him.* Not only the enlisted men, but the officers and knights of all the assembled companies had named him a hero for saving Angelico's sortie. He had already had half a dozen men of title promise their daughters or sisters to him in marriage; who could say how many it would be when the tale spread? It was good food for his heart.

As Michael sat in thought, watching the sun motes fade with the return of the clouds, he considered that he might have been wise to agree to a marriage then and there. Who also could say what his father would do? It made his heart race with anxiety.

But then, his father was always harsher of word than of deed. He had the harder time of the boys, it was true, but he had earned his rank in the officer corps through impeccable command and great exertion of body. His father wanted to dress him down, to hang his position as High Captain over his head and make him suffer shame and fear, to let him know who was really in charge, but his father would not do more than that. His worth as an officer had been proven even this day.

Michael stood as the tent flap opened. Butler, Johan, Towler, and Eduardo the King walked in. With a snap, the high mage gave fire to all the lamps in the tent. The king wore one of his crowns, this one made of iron darkened and polished black. Johan and Eduardo wore makeshift chaplets above blank faces.

"Captain," the king said with flat intonation. Butler and Johan moved to each side of him.

"Your Highness," Michael said, putting his hand to his chest and bowing slightly.

"You disobeyed orders today and led units away from the field of battle," the king said. "What is your defense?"

"I received word that a battalion was marching through the ravine to the north. Our two companies of cavalry and infantry were insufficient to overcome or stall them-"

"You judged them to be, you mean," Johan said.

Michael scowled. "I am explaining to my superior, brother, not my-"

"He is your superior now," the king said. "I have promoted him to general of the army and the legions of west Artalland, as Butler will retire after this campaign."

"I see," Michael said, feeling a drop in his stomach. He looked again at Johan. "Well...sir... I *judged* our forces as insufficient to hold the superior numbers and specialized units-"

"What specialized units?" Johan said.

Michael gritted his teeth. "Heavy cavalry, a cadre of mages, and-"

"The Ferrallese mage corps was on the field. We overcame them using my dragoons, since yours quit the field," Johan said. "Do not lie, Captain."

"There *was* a cadre of mages," Michael said, turning back to his father. "The senior-most mages. The ones we saw wreak havoc in battle at Tolice." He looked to Towler, whose eyes looked remote, as if he was not listening or even looking at him. He got no affirmation from him. "And General Ballaco was leading the sortie."

"More lies?"

"He did not relinquish his sword for surrender, did he? Someone else brought it forth."

"And how do you know that?" Butler said.

Michael felt sweat break out on his face. "Because I shot him with a poison bolt. A dozen men witnessed it. I killed Ballaco D'Ash, saved some four hundred of our men, and won the battle!"

"You won nothing," the king said flatly. "Our *armies* were victorious, not you. And did you not consider that we anticipated such an expedition down that ravine from the Ferrallese?"

"I did not," Michael said, "but if I had, I would not have just left my men to die. A proper officer knows how to adapt to changing battlefield conditions. This was one of those conditions."

"You do not win a battle without losses," Butler said.

"Two companies would be acceptable losses?" Michael said.

"If that was the price of victory, then the price must be paid," the king said.

"We won the battle without those losses, as I have demonstrated," Michael said.

"That was not your decision to make."

Michael took a breath. "I have won you a battle, and I also know this, not just from my studies but from this campaign and the management of General Butler, sir," he nodded to the general, "That victory in the battle may not be enough. You must preserve your fighting force from battle to battle, if you wish to actually conquer. Two companies of dead men would not make for a strong invasion force. You taught me this, sir."

"There will be no invasion," the king said. "We have reached an agreement and a new border will be settled, I'm sure. We go to treat in Ferralla on the morrow."

"I think he took his cavalry into the ravine to rescue his friend," Johan said.

"Angelico?" the king said. Johan nodded.

"He's a good officer," Butler said. "He was a good choice for such a sortie."

"I know Angelico," the king said, grimacing. He straightened up, losing the smallness he seemed to have sitting upon his horse, and looked hard in the eyes of his son. "I find your defense insufficient. I hereby revoke your commission."

"What?" Michael said. He shook his head. Surely he must have misheard.

"I revoke your commission. You are discharged from the service of Artalland, forthwith. You will surrender your banner and cape, your insignias, and your baldric. Your sword, I know, is your own, as is your armor, but you are forbidden to use them in military service."

"You can't be serious."

"I'm deadly serious," the king said. "And I know more of war than you. An army with soldiers who do not follow orders cannot operate as one mind, and cannot win a war where courage is tested. Whether this is from a footman or the highest officer, insubordination cannot be forgiven."

Butler frowned at the king, seemingly unaware of his decision. "Your Highness, don't you consider that a bit harsh? After all, it was just an error in judgment… perhaps just a demotion. Make him a lieutenant and place him in charge of a cavalry detachment, where his skills can be still be put to good use."

"I am already being lenient, general," the king said. As he turned to the mighty girth of Butler, his eyes aflame, he looked every bit the image of Eduardo the Black, the scourge of the Divine Strand. "If he was a footman, he'd be executed. As it is I am merely stripping him of his commission and title-"

"My title?" Michael said.

"The promised estate is for those who serve the kingdom and, perhaps, the empire. Not bad officers that happen to be princes. And yes, I am being lenient, because I believe it was an error in thought and judgment, and while that is less in moral terms than defiance, it is just as bad in terms of outcomes. I have no use for officers that prove that they make bad decisions."

"I don't believe this," Michael said.

"Believe it. Now leave your insignia and get out of our sight. You are no longer a soldier of Artalland. May you find mercy and fortune where you will."

With that, the king turned his back to his son.

"Before I go," Michael said, turning to Towler. "There was a mage in our detachment. Her name was Sharona. If I were her commanding officer, I would consider her for a commendation."

"I will do that for you, Prince," Towler said softly.

Michael nodded to the old mage and pulled his insignia - a blue lacquered pin bearing a pot - from his breastplate and tossed it on the table. He walked out into a new rain, light and cool, which had not put a damper on the celebrations. In the west the clouds glowed with the sunset, lighting the mountains in a multitude of shades. He took off his helm and looked up at the dark clouds, thankful for the cool drops on his face.

*

Michael tied down his tack carefully. It was, he thought, a pitiful amount of possession for a prince, but then almost everything he used had been property of the army - his tent, his pack mule, his cot and furniture, his wagon, and even his cloak of bold blue, the sign of his house and legion, which would be getting a new banner soon. His armor was stacked behind the cantile, an odd pile of now dirty steel.

He heard footsteps in the mud and turned to see Angelico walking toward him, unarmored but still belted.

"Where are you headed, sir?"

Michael forced a smile at him. "Home. I've been… discharged from my duty."

Angelico frowned, his eyes trembling with the light of a nearby campfire. "That can't be. You won the day, sir, you-"

"It is true, my friend. Not sir, anymore, by the way."

"Your Highness?"

Michael laughed.

"Sir," Angelico went on, "I'll resign in protest. I can get the entire cavalry-"

"No," Michael said sternly. "No, I will take no man's career and prospects with me from this camp. Merely my own."

"But if you were reinstated-"

"I won't be. You know my father."

"Not as well as you do."

"True. Don't tell the men until the morrow. I want nothing to spoil their well-earned satisfaction. And Natino, my squire," Michael went on, "will need someone new to apprentice with."

"You're still gentry," Angelico said. "You can still have a squire."

Michael shook his head. "I can't afford him."

"The prince cannot afford a servant?"

"My promissory title is forfeit. I am lucky I didn't take any debts out on it. I will have to rely on the royal household now." He bit his lip. "And find my own future."

"You'll always have a place in my house if you want it. My youngest sister is eligible. There is plenty of space in our lands and manor-"

"Allow me to refuse you today."

"I owe you a debt," Angelico said. "A steep one."

"You owe that debt to your fellows, not to me. One thing my father said today is at least true: it is the army that wins the battle, not the commander. Pay the men back well. Keep them safe."

"I will, sir."

Michael winced as he stepped into the stirrup.

"Did you ever tend to that arrow wound?" Angelico said.

"Yes," Michael said, gritting his teeth and swinging into the saddle. "Hurts worse now that the arrow's gone. Luckily it wasn't deep."

"I can have a mage heal you. A few of them know how to do it."

"Those services are reserved for soldiers. Now go have a drink for me."

Michael clicked his tongue and Calot set off slowly. He looked back to see Angelico standing in the path, and waved to him. Angelico trotted off, wrapping his blue cloak about himself. Michael let Calot walk of his own accord up the path and under a low hanging oak. At the end of the path, among the entrenchments and camp fortifications, he saw a shadowy figure. Instinctively he reached for his sword and loosened it in its scabbard.

The figure was holding a lamp and sitting upon a horse, a long cloak over its head holding off the rain. As he got closer, Michael could see the unmistakable pointed black beard of his brother, Johan.

"What do you want from me now, brother?" Michael said, sliding his sword safely back into its scabbard.

"Just to see my brother safely on the road."

"To gloat?"

"When have I ever gloated, save when we were children?"

Michael answered with silence and gave Calot a slight squeeze. As he passed by, Johan reached out a gloved hand grabbed the reins.

"I try to warn you, Michael, but you don't ever listen."

"Pray tell me, brother, what I should have listened to this time."

"The quaver in our father's aging voice. The croak in old Butler's voice. The subtle, soft breathing of Towler."

"I should have listened to the old men?"

"You should have listened to their age, Michael. Old men are hard and stubborn, set in their ways and they don't like to be countermanded. Perhaps if you had held your tongue this morning your stunt would have been reluctantly rewarded. Now you head home, to shame."

"This isn't gloating?"

"I'm trying to teach you something, Michael."

"Why? I'm out of the service. I have nothing to give for the kingdom. Or at least, nothing I am permitted to give."

"You may be free of the military, but you are still a prince of Artalland. Nobody can strip you of that inheritance."

"The younger prince. I have no inheritance, besides by grace or by… some other event."

"The future is uncertain. Death is always a closer friend than you realize, even outside of this business of war."

"You're thinking of Tasolo?"

"Yes. Illness comes to even the strong. Do not forget him."

"I cannot forget my younger brother."

"Michael, did it occur to you that I could have been slain today?"

Michael thought for a moment. "I suppose I always know that's a possibility, but you're too good to be slain. Too valuable for ransom. And you never lead from the front."

"It is irresponsible to lead from the front. I have a duty to minimize my risk in the pursuit of my manly duties. And you do too, for you know that I could die, and since I am yet childless, you would be king. Or father could have been slain, and then your position in the house all the more relevant."

Michael said, "I shall be safe in Calasora now, at least."

Johan chuckled. "Oh no. The battlefield is indeed safer than the capital for you. On the battlefield, you are at least competent. Among the gentry, you are… Politics are dangerous, brother." Johan took a slow breath. "I said old men are hard, but they are also wise. Butler is not a fool. He considered the press down the ravine among possibilities, as he assumes the enemy has the same knowledge of the terrain as himself. That gambit was stacked in our favor. By sending two of our best companies - and indeed they are the best, Michael, for in the ways of war you are far from inept - he could counter a sortie. If none came, they had a clear auxiliary objective. Did you not discern this in the planning meeting?"

"Truthfully, no."

"You were too busy objecting to the plan to consider its merits," Johan said. "I'm sorry for being harsh, but that is how it is."

"He knew Angelico's companies would be wiped out."

"It was a possibility, yes."

"I couldn't allow that. I won't sacrifice my men like that."

"Then it is good you are exiting warfare now. Sacrifices are sometimes necessary. You cannot think that the men beneath you are as valuable as yourself."

"What?" Michael said, suddenly raising his voice. "How could you say that?"

"Because it is true. You are a prince, they are noble sons and mostly commoners. To secure the future of the kingdom, it must remain in the hands of those most competent to guide the kingdom, which is us. To deny your importance is to hand Artalland over to tyrants and fools. You *must always* do what is necessary to hold power, lest it fall into hands of lesser character."

"Sending my friends to die doesn't sound like good character to me."

"See, there it is. These men are not your friends, Michael! They cannot be your friends, for they can never be your equal. They are soldiers, sworn to do what is necessary to preserve their king and, therefore, their country."

"So the end justifies the means."

"If it doesn't justify the means, what does? You are a grown man, Michael. It is time to put childhood ideals of being righteous behind you, and focus on the outcomes of your actions."

"The outcomes of my actions won the battle tonight!"

"The battle was won before the first horn call. Before the first arrow flew."

Michael scoffed. "My actions saved a large part of my legion."

"At the risk of the entire army, and therefore our family and our country. I need you to think like a king."

Silently, Michael pulled Johan's hands away from the reins.

"Wait, Michael."

"No."

"You must not leave alone, without a retinue to protect you."

"I require no protection, brother."

"Please, I have something I would ask you to do."

Michael stopped and looked back. Johan pulled a roll of paper from the inside of his cloak and handed it to him. "Please give this to Julia when you see her. And tell her I miss her."

Michael nodded, stuffed the scroll into a pocket in his coat, and slowly rode out past the makeshift battlements.

"Preserve yourself, brother!" Johan called after him. Michael waved a slow hand in return.

III: Strange Company

Michael regretted his choice to leave during the night almost immediately. The wind whipped at his cloak and the rain blew into his face, as well as the face of Calot, who he began to feel quite sorry for. The quilted jacket he wore was useless against the chill that seemed to soak through him, and the moon behind the clouds did little to light his way. He relied on the ever-marching tall grass to his right to guide his way on the road.

Worse than that, however, was the solitude, and the time it afforded him to relive every moment of the day, faces of dead and living men alike flowing across his thoughts in the darkness. This began to disturb him after some miles, so he got down to light a lamp, which was difficult in the dripping rain. When at last the wick took flame he hung the lamp beside his horse on a small lamp-pole, which dispelled some of the darkness, though it did nothing to make him feel less lonely.

"It is a cruel thing, to leave a man alone with his thoughts after a battle," he said to Calot. "Maybe that's why we're so quick to celebrate being alive."

Michael began to replay the events of the day over and over in his mind, wondering how he could have prevented what happened to him. He wondered what he should have said, or what he should have done differently. Always, given the size of Ballaco's force, he came back to the conclusion that the battle would have been lost.

Ballaco, with a full battalion of mixed units, would have come out of the ravine well north of the forward camp, but it would have been higher ground and well-covered. He would have easily routed Michael's reserves, which were almost entirely infantry and of a similar number. From there the general would have pinched the battlefield, and perhaps even captured the king, though he thought it more likely that his father would have seen the maneuver and surrendered, knowing the day was lost. He was a stubborn man, but no fool.

He *had* won the battle, but… why did Ballaco send so many men down the ravine? Or, why were there only two companies sent against him? Things didn't add up. Ballaco had to have known what he was doing, what was waiting for him in the ravine.

At last Michael tired of his own thoughts and rested Calot beneath some drooping beeches on a little hill, where the ground was almost dry. He first thought he was too miserable to sleep, but eventually, the fatigue of the battle, and the ache in his side, made him forget the infinite turns of fate in his head, and he nodded off.

A day and a half after leaving the army, Michael had come upon a little village, nestled in a sparse wood with good vineyards and fields all around. There was no inn as such there, but a homely landowner put him up for a night, recognizing him as the prince. The next day he came upon another town, called Gabora Minor, which was busy and full of people, who let him know that if there ever was a Gabora Major it was long lost in the hearty oak woods of the country upland from the village.

There he rested in a raucous inn called the Mottled Wyrm, which had comfortable beds. It seemed that in Gabora Minor nobody recognized him as a prince of Artalland, for nobody gave him any deference. Being raised a prince and then spending his youth in the military as an officer, this behavior was strange to him. People did not step out of his way when he went on a walk, nor did they make any offer of service without him asking first. The local stable-keeper, in fact, told him to come back later, as he was too busy to fuss over yet another horse. And everywhere, people wanted to haggle, demanding outrageous sums for simple services.

Michael decided to stay there an extra day, finding the strange behavior also strangely refreshing. He actually began to enjoy (as he admitted to the bartender of the Mottled Wyrm, who did not seem to care) that nobody recognized him. He felt relief from those days detached from the army and the shame of his dressing down by his father. In anonymity, his shame was at least his alone. His whole life felt empty too, for before he had always filled it with the life of military officership, and yet the emptiness was likewise refreshing.

He found himself, therefore, doing something he had never before permitted himself to do, which was wasting an afternoon sitting on a mound of turf beneath a tree, reading a book of fiction and folktales. As he turned the dirty pages (the book was borrowed from the innkeeper, a jolly old woman who collected fiction) he found himself feeling strangely happy.

"Oh, that's a fun one."

Michael squinted and looked up to see a dark-haired woman standing nearby wearing a simple dress, holding the reins of a large warhorse.

"Yes," Michael said, shutting the book for a moment and reading the title of *The Lays of the Old Wyrms.* "I seldom read fiction. My father always said it was a waste of time and rot for the mind."

"That one's not fiction."

"It's about dragons and faeries."

"Which are both real." Sharona sighed and smiled. "I especially like the stories with the dragon Garamesh. Oh, and don't gentlemen usually stand for a lady?"

"What?" Michael said. He finally processed what she had sad and stood up hastily, brushing the grass off his trousers. "Yes, the… dragon." Michael coughed. "Do you require assistance?"

"No. I just hadn't expected to see you sitting under a tree reading." She squinted for a moment and looked to the west. She said softly to herself, "Where was I expecting you?"

Michael stepped forward and suddenly recognized the face. "Sharona, isn't it?"

"It is I. In the flesh," she said airily, her face unreadable.

"I didn't recognize you without your armor on. What are you doing here? You should be attached to the mage corps, not be on leave. Not yet, anyway."

"I was sacked."

"What?"

"I was sacked," she said loudly.

Michael shook his head. "You lost your commission, you mean?"

"Yes, that's what they told me. I was losing my commission," Sharona said. "Now, we were talking about dragons..."

"I recommended you for a commendation," Michael said, feeling perplexed. "What happened?"

"I don't know... Someone or other came and told me I was released from duty, handed me a sack of silver, and told me to go home. So that is what I am doing."

"You seem rather ambivalent about your situation."

Sharona shrugged. "I think I already did what I was meant to do with the army, but I still need to-"

"Wait," Michael said, looking at the horse behind her. "What are you doing with that horse?"

"Rabble-rouser? Yes, I did rename him. I'm riding him. Well, not currently, obviously, but within a larger frame of time I am riding him as a means of transport."

"I mean, you own that destrier?"

"Can you really *own* a horse?" Sharona said, raising her eyebrows.

"Yes, you can," Michael said. "What I mean is, did you bring that horse with you when you were admitted to the corps?"

"No, he was given to me."

Michael shook his head. "No. That horse belongs to the Artalland army. It was assigned to you for your use as a soldier. You *stole* that horse."

"Can it really be stealing if you can't *own* a horse?"

Michael blinked slowly. "Yes, Sharona." He sighed. "Don't worry, I'll smooth it out somehow when I get back to Calasora."

"Oh, that would be appreciated."

"Consider it payment for what you did in the battle. All the same, you really ought not let that horse be seen around any cavalry officers. Nobody with the right eye will mistake a destrier for a traveling horse."

"I don't expect to see many officers. Now, we were talking about *dragons*. I have an interesting story that I should tell you. You see-"

"You know," Michael said. "I ought to get going. I have some errands to attend to." He turned to walk away and gritted his teeth as he paused. He took a long breath, feeling a nagging inside him, then said. "Should I gather that you are traveling alone?"

"I am."

Michael grumbled softly. "Where are you headed? I'll escort you there. You ought not travel alone on the road."

"Why? You're alone."

"I'm a man and trained soldier. I'm in no danger of passing highwaymen."

"Neither am I. I can crack men's femur bones, remember?"

"Are you carrying chicken bones?"

"No, but I have other tools."

"Well, if you want an escort I am at your service, such as it is. Where are you headed?"

She looked away for a long moment and frowned, as if thinking or, as Michael half-thought, listening to an inaudible voice.

"Colasora," she said.

"Fortuitous," Michael said flatly. "I shall escort you there."

*

The sun was hot as they let the horses take their own paces along the dusty road. Sharona wore a piece of cloth over her head loosely to keep the light out of her eyes. For lack of a traveling hat, Michael wore his helm with his visor up, but no padding beneath. He debated in his mind whether it made things better or worse, as the metal began to get quite hot.

"So," Sharona said. "We never finished our conversation about dragons. There was-"

"What was there to finish? Dragons aren't real."

"You really ought to travel more."

"Well, have you seen one?"

"I have, as a matter of fact. Well, sort of. I was trying to explain... but I've definitely seen a few drakes. Those are small dragons, very beast-like. They can't really talk. Not like the true dragons, like Tathanon, or Iodemus, or Garamesh."

"And where exactly have you seen a drake?"

"In the Dobo Wold, of course."

"You've been there?"

"I am *from* there."

"What the hell are you doing in Artalland?"

"I am riding a horse beside a prince."

"What prompted you to cross the Divine Spires and come to Artalland, then?"

"I had a dream."

Michael scoffed. "We all have dreams."

Sharona narrowed her eyes contemptuously. "In it, a dragon told me I needed to come here to discover who I am."

Michael smiled at her. "You don't know who you are? I thought you were Sharona."

"Well, I admit I thought I knew who I was. I'm not an orphan, if you were wondering."

"I wasn't, but that's good, I suppose," Michael said. He took his helmet off suddenly, feeling awkward. "Orphans are a terrible tragedy."

"What an odd thing to say," Sharona said, frowning.

"So… What made you want to join the mage corps, once you arrived in Artalland?"

"Well, I lit a lamp with magic, and someone saw me and asked if I was an officer in the mage corps. So I found the Calasora legion and signed up. I thought maybe that was what mages do in your country."

"The few we can find we try to press into service, it's true," Michael said. "I hear the gifts are thinning out as time goes on."

"That's because this world is slowly dying."

Michael laughed. "Is that all?"

"Oh no, that's not all, but that is why magic is seen less in people. The once bright Faylands are beginning to dry up. The eternal dream is giving way to the mundane, not the magical."

Michael was silent for a moment. "What happens when it dries up?"

"The world dies. Or it will be dead by that time."

"What happens to us?"

"We'll be dead by then, I'm sure. It'll take a long time to dry up totally, I think."

"I mean, what will happen to *people* when the world dies."

"Nothing," Sharona said, with a shrug. "The world will be dead, not the people. It will be mundane and unchanging."

"It changes now?"

"Yes, in subtle ways everywhere, in big ways in some places. In the past, the world was constantly being reformed by the twists in the Eternal Dream and the dreamers still in it." Sharona looked over her shoulder at nothing in particular. "I've been there, you know. The Fay Lands."

"Have you?"

"Yes. The people in my village seem to think it made me crazy."

Michael was about to say, *They're right,* but thought better of it. "Let's pause here a moment. There are some people up the way."

"How do you know?"

Michael pointed over the trees. "A bit of smoke. We're close to Landera, but not too close. Could be a bandit or two."

Michael reached down and retrieved his crossbow. He set about loading it.

"You don't have to worry about that, your highness."

"Better safe than sorry."

"I mean don't worry, I'll protect you."

"I need no protection."

"Then why have the crossbow and the sword?"

Michael laughed.

They saw across the road a broken wagon, and Michael put out a hand to still Sharona.

"Aha!" he whispered. "It *is* a bandit."

"It looks like a broken wagon," Sharona said at full volume.

Michael shushed her. "It's an old scam. You pause and get off your horse to help the poor merchant with his broken wagon, and they jump on your horse and rob you."

"Oh," Sharona said, raising an eyebrow. "Wonder why they don't just shoot us with arrows."

"Because bandits are usually rubbish when it comes to actual fighting. I thought you said you'd traveled."

Sharona shrugged.

Michael took out his crossbow and led them up the road. He paused when an old, dirty man stepped out into the road from the wagon, waving. Michael shouldered his crossbow and took aim, not at the old man, but at a shadow in the trees above him.

With a snap, the bolt flew and struck something. A man screamed and fell from the tree down into the road. He rolled over and pushed himself away from the road, a broken bolt lodged in his ribcage.

"Flee now, and I will count the execution of one of you as sufficient," Michael called. He put the crank back on his crossbow and began spanning it. The old man was frozen in the road with fright. The other men hidden in the bushes were not, and they leapt out, well away from where they had set their trap.

A few bolts flew past Michael and Sharona as the men from the bushes rushed forward with swords and clubs. Michael calmly loaded his crossbow as they ran. Before he could pop a bolt in, he looked up at a terrible noise.

The bandits were rolling on the ground crying in pain. Michael looked at Sharona, who was glassy-eyed and mumbling incoherently. Her horse was moving anxiously. The old man in front of the wagon went running into the brush.

"Let's go!" Michael said.

Sharona shook her head, looked at Michael with bright eyes, then followed him down the path as he galloped among and over the bandits, who were crying and writhing on the ground.

A half mile or so up the road, they slowed.

"I told you I would protect you," Sharona said.

"I have to say, that was impressive, whatever you did."

"I made them feel like swarms of bees were stinging them. It's very painful, but they *were* trying to rob us, yes?"

"Yes, they clearly were. And probably would have slit our throats if they'd had the chance. I'll notify the sheriff in Landera so he can clear them out."

"What about the one you shot?"

"He's a criminal."

"So am I, you said."

Michael chuckled softly. "Not the best comparison. You're a lady. Well… a woman."

"Small wonder you aren't married with a tongue like that."

Michael looked at her, confused. Sharona was looking away, a half-smile on her placid face.

*

Calasora was a massive city, spanning two sides of the great river Tallaros some miles before it bubbled into a wide delta and emptied into the South Sea. The two halves of the city, West and East Calasora, were joined by great stone bridges held above the slow-moving river by columns of black basalt. From the river, canals and waterways went into the city, supplying fresh water for the many public fountains that served both rich and poor. At the center of the city, standing from the western shore to an island in the river, to a temple on the eastern shore, stood the great Citadel of Artifia, which served as palace, cathedral to the goddess Artifia, and fortress to the royal family of Harthino, along with the rich denizens that inhabited the mansions that surrounded it.

The west bank of the city had also over the years come to be called the "City of Walls," or more affectionately, "the Onion City," on account of its long succession of defensive walls. Each of these walls was built during a different period in the city, and reflected different tastes and defensive designs. As the city grew out past a wall, a new one was built to contain it. At five walls the attempts had stopped, and the city just went sprawling over the rocky countryside and to the other side of the river, which had its own (smaller) fortress and wall that was usually entitled to whatever family was most politically connected at the time to the royal line.

The gates of the walls were offset from each other, but a wide avenue wound between them. It was on this avenue, and approaching the first gate, that Michael finally decided he could part ways with Sharona without feeling a loss of his honor.

"So, where are you headed?" Michael said.

"Calasora."

"We are here."

"Alright then."

Michael grumbled. "Where in the city do you need to be?"

"I don't know."

"Why don't you know? Do you just not know where to go? I know the city well. Tell me what you seek and I shall tell you where to go."

"I don't seek anything in particular."

"Then why did you come here?"

"Because you were coming here."

Michael slapped his own face. "So you had no reason to be here?"

"I had an excellent reason to be here. I'm here because you are here. Because you need my protection."

"I don't need your protection."

Sharona laughed. "Of course you do. Why else would I be here?"

"You're not making any sense!"

"Of course not. You don't *make* sense, you have sense."

"Artifia, grant me patience!" Michael sighed and turned to Sharona. She wore a half-smile, as if she was getting something over on him. "What makes you think *you* need to protect *me?*"

"Because I wouldn't be here if you didn't need me. Didn't I just say that?"

"What…" Calot twisted as Michael tensed in frustration. "What made you think you ought to come here, and that I needed you?"

"Didn't you answer your own question?"

"Grim's bones. I have some kind of luck. Why did I have to run into you under that tree?"

"There's no such thing as luck, Michael, just as there is no such thing as coincidence. I ran into you under that tree for a reason."

Michael clicked his teeth. "That reason being I require protection."

"It's my assumption, just as I was placed by you in the battle for your protection. It could be something else, but that will become obvious when it arrives. I just know that I was placed by that tree as surely as the farmer was placed in Garamesh's cave."

"He walked into the dragon's cave of his own volition."

"False."

"I just read the story, you know."

"Not closely," Sharona said. "You're a vision of a man, but you have trouble seeing."

"Nevermind," Michael said softly. He urged his horse forward, and Sharona kept pace. "I know of an inn up the way here that's rather quiet and safe. I'll pay to put you up for a few nights, and you can decide what it is you need to do from there."

"Alright, but I'll pay. I'm no pauper. I can make money fairly easily too, if needed."

"Suit yourself."

"Of course I suit myself. What would I do if I didn't?"

Michael shook his head and grumbled. As they ambled between the houses, he drew out the sealed scroll addressed to Julia, stamped with Johan's personal signet of a scorpion.

"What's that?" Sharona asked.

"A letter from my brother to his betrothed." Michael looked at the rolled paper and chewed his lip.

"Curious what it says?"

"Yes, of course. Who isn't curious what's in a sealed letter?"

"Me."

"You say that," Michael said, looking to Sharona and her calm, generous smirk. "Actually, I might believe that you alone aren't held by the curiosity of secrets, if you were to say such a thing."

"Oh, but I don't say that. I said I wasn't curious about sealed letters. When is the last time a secret was put to letter?"

Michael chuckled. "You aren't noble."

"I know. I'm virtuous. There's a difference, you know." Sharona paused and tapped her lips. "I think I could reseal the letter if you are indeed so curious. I know a little spell for moving things backward a few minutes."

"Handy, but no," Michael said. "If there is something worth knowing in this letter, aside from private salutations, Julia will tell me. We spent our childhoods together and are friends, of a sort."

"Why aren't *you* betrothed to her?"

Michael paused and gazed at Sharona. "I don't think I understand."

Sharona raised her eyebrows, giving her calm face a frightened expression. "You are friends, grew up together you say, and you clearly share confidence. You hadn't thought of courting her?"

"It doesn't work like that in Artalland," Michael said. "Except maybe with peasants."

"Well, who are *you* engaged to?"

"Nobody. Yet. Though I've had several offers, I think I shall find most of those maidens suddenly unavailable."

"You'd think the prospect of marrying a prince would make them available."

"That depends on which prince. A second son who has had his titles and pensions stripped? Not much value there, even in terms of prestige."

They were silent for a minute or two, Michael refusing to look over at the mage.

"You never asked me if *I* was engaged," Sharona said. "Isn't it good manners here to return conversation questions as such?"

"Among equals," Michael said. He grumbled to himself, then said, "Who are you engaged to?"

"Nobody," Sharona said.

"Then why did you make me ask?"

"I didn't *make* you do anything." She sighed. "I'm afraid my father will not be pleased. He thought my standards were already too high, and now I am talking to a prince."

Michael shook his head and sighed.

*

The castle, as grand as it was and as filled as it was with servants and ministers, felt cold and lonely to Michael without his father, brother, and friends-in-arms hanging about. Not for the first time he missed his mother, if for no other reason than he knew she was somebody who would speak to him with love, regardless of what had happened following the last battle with the Ferrallese forces.

He made up his mind early in the morning to go hunting, favoring the warm spring weather and wishing to leave the ancient walls of Artifia's citadel. When he exited the courtyard for the stables, his great hunting crossbow on his shoulder, he found Sharona standing idly by, playing a card game by herself on an upturned crate.

"Sharona," Michael said. "I expected you would be on your way by now."

"To where, exactly?" Sharona said, puzzling over the face-up cards in her solitaire game.

"To your home."

"When did I say that I would be heading home?"

"Yesterday," Michael said, gritting his teeth.

"I said nothing of the sort. Your memory ought to be better than that."

Michael took a slow breath, trying to calm himself. "Why are you here now?"

"I decided that you still need me."

"I do not."

"I don't believe you are in the best position to judge. Hence I will continue to protect you until such time as I feel that you do not need me, or…" She considered a card move, wrinkling her brow. "Or circumstances change"

"I *am* in the best position to judge."

"Then you have discovered who the traitor is. Are we off to rouse him?" Sharona stood up and adjusted an old sword that was belted around her simple dress.

"What? No. I was about to go hunting. Now go home." Michael turned to walk to the stables, but stopped as Sharona followed him.

"Do I have to make the castle guard lock you up?"

"Are you actually *going* to have the guard lock me up?"

Michael groaned in frustration and continued toward the stables. Outside of them, he ran into Guissali, a knight and one of the house retainers, who smiled broadly as he approached.

"Your Highness! It is good to see you home and in one piece!"

Michael smiled back. "I wish it were in better circumstances."

"What do you mean?"

"Nothing," Michael said. "Will you be riding with us today?"

"With your permission."

"Granted. It will be good to have a friendly face about."

Guissali nudged Michael in the ribs. "Speaking of friendly faces, there was a young lady looking for you. I sent her to find you."

"Sharona?"

"That's the one. She seemed rather keen on you, sire."

Michael cleared his throat. "Yes… well, work on improving your vetting, Gui." He nodded behind him, to where Sharona stood, a few paces back, looking up at the clouds.

"Did I do something wrong?" Guissali said.

Michael sighed. "No, friend. Don't consider it further."

Guissali watched Sharona a moment, then laughed. "I understand. Don't worry. You're the prince. She'll forgive a slip of the tongue." Guissali's large hand patted Michael on the back as they walked into the stables.

Michael picked out his favorite hunting horse, a roan he named Tutt, and with the help of a servant began saddling him and setting up his gear.

He and Guissali rode slowly to the front gate, where the huntmaster, an old war hero with one eye named Sotoro, waited with his hounds. Sharona was already there, a few paces away from the old man and watching the hounds nervously.

"Who's the wench, my magnanimous lord?" Sotoro said, his high voice creaking like old leather.

"A mage. Call her my bodyguard, I suppose," Michael said.

"Ha!" Guissali said. "This is a chance for her to see your prowess, my prince."

"She saw my prowess in battle," Michael said.

"Ah! Then this is merely a social opportunity. Whose daughter is she?"

Michael shook his head silently.

Sotoro smiled. "You have good tastes, your beneficent grace. Your servant Sotoro, loyal to the last, approves."

"It's not like that, huntmaster."

"Of course it isn't, your high gracefulness. I wasn't insinuating anything improprietous, my great and powerful prince."

"Enough with the groveling, Sot. Have you a good line on the game today?"

"Most good, High Lord. Good deer, good foxes. Good boar too, mighty one."

"Well… good, then. Lead on."

They followed Sotoro out of the castle and down to the river, where they took a path that wound north, past rows of houses that grew steadily newer and of lesser construction skill, and then passed alongside a stone wall meant to defend an assault from the river. Eventually, they came to a sparse wood, well maintained, and met another retinue of the huntmaster's helpers, as well as a few soldiers. They were sitting in the back of a wagon, and this Michael followed further into the trees.

"Did you deliver your letter yet?" Sharona said.

"No," Michael said.

"Why is that?"

"I haven't had the time."

"Which explains why we are hunting, yes? We are in desperate need of food!"

"Very funny," Michael said.

"Is it because you don't want to tell her you got sacked?"

"Of course not. That will be news eventually anyway. Probably already is, the way my father runs the pigeons."

"Ah," Sharona said. "I think I understand."

"Do you?"

"Yes. It is like a child that stays away from home when he knows he's done something wrong. The punishment is coming no matter what, but it feels better in the moment to avoid it than to take it on."

"It's nothing like that."

"Then let's go deliver the letter."

"You wouldn't be coming with me if I did," Michael said.

At last, they reached the royal hunting grounds, a wide stretch of meadows and woods near the great river. After watering the dogs, Sotoro unleashed them. He kicked his horse into a gallop, following them a dozen or so yards to their right. Michael rode straight on, dashing ahead of them to intercept the prey they scared up.

The assistants to the huntmaster had already stationed themselves further up and caught a few quail as the dogs snarled and snapped at a covey that flew up from some bushes. For the better part of half an hour, they followed the two hounds around in a wide circle, but no larger game presented themselves. Michael decided to go further upland, in hope of finding a velvet stag, but after an hour of riding, he acquiesced to watering Tutt at a creek and resting, finding his himself too inwardly distracted to search for the signs of deer.

The day wore on, at last they set out on the trek back to the citadel, no big game in tow.

"No food today, then," Sharona said as they ambled beside the river.

"Well, we got some quail. Good eating for the huntsmen." Michael took a long drink of water and looked up at an overhanging pine tree, leaning precariously to one side.

"You've been quiet and far too polite. You seem distracted," Sharona said.

"I am. Something you said, maybe. About a traitor. I keep thinking about it. In truth, I considered it during the battle but put it out of my mind once the fighting got on."

"Oh yes, Go on, who do you think it is?"

"I don't know yet, but as my mind replays the events of the battle, I can't help but think it likely there was one. There's no way Ballaco would have committed an entire battalion to a sortie down that northern ravine, unless he knew the resistance would be mild and the prize ripe. I doubt he even knew of the ravine, and certainly I find it unlikely he knew of the position of our forward camp. I think our camp placement, even, was a weakness. So somebody had to tell him what we were doing."

Michael paused and looked to the sun in the west. "He was using our plan against us. He had to know of it ahead of time. What makes *you* suspect a traitor?"

Sharona shrugged and tossed an errant hair out of her face. "I just figured you wouldn't have been sacked unless you knew something you weren't supposed to know."

"Good point, though why not Angelico? He kept his commission." Michael shook his head. "I can't see who would have betrayed us."

"I'm sure you can. Unless he is invisible," Sharona giggled. "The army *is* a big group, though."

"Yes," Michael said. "But if you consider timing… The plan wasn't disseminated until right before the battle to the other officers. It had to be somebody in top command, or else Ballaco was a very lucky guesser indeed."

"Well, I say it was general whats-his-name, since the king has no reason to lose a war, and by extension, his sons don't."

"Or Towler."

"Towler is far too honest for that," Sharona said. "Not ambitious enough, and he's terrible at keeping secrets."

"He is?"

"Oh yes, he told me all about the battle plan."

"That rat. It had to be him," Michael said, sitting up in the saddle and petting Tutt nervously.

"Or the general."

"Butler has always been loyal. Plus his daughter is Julia and engaged to the crown prince." Michael pumped his fist. "Damn that they won't be back for weeks. They'll be in Ferralla negotiating with Queen Alanrae for terms of surrender and peace. And that snake Towler will be there. Who knows what he'll be able to accomplish?"

"I know what." Sharona shook her head. "He's a good mage and I'm sure he can accomplish a lot, but I don't think he's a traitor."

"He's the most likely, the weakest link in loyalty." Michael took a deep breath. "I'm going to have to travel to Ferralla, and quickly."

IV: Turns

Michael's boots echoed in the gallery, washing his ears with sound as his eyes took in the familiar sights of the citadel, fresh and sharp amid the churning worry in his stomach. Great windows of colored glass stood high above, drowning the hallway in warm light. He passed by the portraits and statues of his ancestors, tributaries to the great river that was his family's passage through time. The Third Dominion had grown its order and passed away, the Divine Empire had been shattered irreparably to bring about the Fourth Dominion, and yet the house of Harthino and their great citadel, their great city, had endured, its leaders growing from governors to great kings.

Still, Michael felt saddened by watching the immaculate faces pass by, for of those ancestors but a few had been second sons. His face might grace its own gallery, but it would be in a different fief, in a different gallery, for proud sons of a nobleman, not a king. At the same time, he felt an obligation to those faces, especially those second and third sons, for they had carried their lineage forward always to the next generation without fail. When Michael thought of the traitor in the midst of the Harthino house and the probability of treason growing from a seed of mere possibility to a near certainty the more he thought about it, he desired most to see one more face added to the gallery of kings, whichever son should have it. He also knew he loved his brother, and that was a bracing thought to him.

At last Michael turned a corner and came to the cluster of offices he was seeking. Two servants were quietly talking but shut their mouths when Michael turned the corner. He passed into the room of Lord Magutus, his father's chief minister of domestic operation. The old man was writing in a ledger at a desk below one of the large windows that framed the immense library of Harthino, depicting in small stained glass the twelve gods in poses befitting their domains. He looked up as Michael entered.

"Your Highness," he said coolly, standing and giving a slight bow as Michael stopped in front of the desk. "I was wondering when you were going to come see me." He straightened his finely embroidered robes, which hung loosely over him, tailored for when he was a larger man.

"I trust that our books are in order?"

"If you'd like to order an audit, all will be in its place."

"Good. Any events whilst I was away?"

"Plenty, but none that concern you. Drama with employees ought to be beneath the concern of the monarchy - at least, I aim to make it so."

"Good. I am leaving for Ferralla post-haste. I wanted to inform you that I will be gone some time, and will likely return with my father and brother after we have seen to the surrender of Ferralla."

"Ferralla is surrendering? The pigeon was true, then," Magutus said, walking over to a bookshelf and pulling from it a small slip of paper. "My message was rain-soaked and blurry, but when you did not formally announce victory upon your arrival... when you refused company I thought that...." He shook his head. "No matter. You will be assisting in the negotiations, then?"

Michael stared at the slip in the old man's hands, feeling his stomach churn slightly.

"What else did the message say?" Michael asked.

Magutus shook his head. "It said to wait for further instructions for a victory parade. Why?"

Michael chewed his cheek. Had the message been sent prior to him being stripped of his commission? Did it lack this detail, or was Magutus hiding what he knew?

"Just curious if my father had any message for me."

"Alas, no," Magutus said.

"I see. I must leave now. I must trust the operation of the city and kingdom to you and the high court for the next fortnight, perhaps longer."

Magutus nodded. As Michael turned to leave, the old man spoke again. "Why, then, did my lord return to the city? Just to check on me?"

"Yes," Michael said. "My father and brother are indisposed to check on the care of the kingdom."

"I see. May you find death only in victory, High captain."

"That's not necessary."

"I understand," Magutus said softly, bowing.

"Of course you do, or you would have saluted me properly when I entered. Farewell, Magutus, and remember that I can count."

"Of course, your highness, of course."

Michael stopped and turned back. He drew out the letter for Julia and rolled it in his hands. "I have one more thing for you. Please deliver this to Lady Julia. It is from the crown prince."

Magutus held up his hands lightly. "She would be most distressed to have me deliver such a thing, to take on your obligation while you are still here. Please, allow me for my own sake to decline your request."

"I suppose I shall," Michael said with a sigh. "Be well, Lord. And count to your heart which relations are dearest, for we will likely be possessing new lands next month."

"And you, my prince - Stay safe." The minister bowed low and Michael swept out of the room.

*

Michael waited outside the door to Julia's apartments; her attendants insisted that she needed a few minutes to be ready to receive a prince. He took from his pocket a gold coin and began flipping it absentmindedly as he leaned against the wall. The rhythm was somewhat soothing, ticking away the painful seconds in waiting to inevitably explain his shame to Julia.

Flick... and catch… and turn…. and flick...and catch… and turn.

Perhaps he could avoid telling her, since formal news had not been proclaimed. Just tell her he came to check on her and the city.

Flick… and catch… and turn… and flick… and catch.

But then she was always good and knowing when he was lying and of course, being Butler's daughter, she would find out eventually and scold him for his dishonesty.

Flick… and catch….

Maybe women didn't find as much shame in these things. But had he actually done anything to be ashamed of?

Flick… and catch… and turn…

Of course, the traitor might have put his father up to it. Butler had stuck up for him…

Flick… and catch…. and turn… and flick…. and…

Michael stared around, bewildered. Where had the coin gone? He looked on the floor, mad that he had not heard the coin dropping. Then, he looked up again and saw it, hovering right in front of his face, not turning, but bouncing slightly. He reached out to grab it, but it flew away from his hand, to his right. He tried again, and again the coin flew away. Michael flung his hands out to grasp it, but it kept moving away.

"What in the high hell?" he said aloud to himself. He heard a soft giggle and turned to see Sharona, wearing black trousers, boots, and a blouse, walking down the hallway without making a sound, holding a gold coin in front of her. She moved it around and the coin in front of Michael moved too. Then she closed her hand and Michael's coin fell to the floor, tinkling loudly.

"Who let you in the citadel?"

"Oh, I had Guissali vouch for me at the gate. Your retainer is an excellent judge of character, I find."

"I'll question him on that."

"When are we leaving? I already packed and paid my bill at the inn, which was much more expensive than you let on."

"I would have paid your tab, had you just gone home," Michael said quietly.

"I can pay my own way. I mended a few pots and pans for the inn-keeper, and he was most grateful. I also enchanted the boils off of his son's back. Very nasty, but worth an Argent." She flipped the coin in the air and snapped her fingers. It burst into flame for a moment before smoking and landing in her palm. She juggled the hot coin awkwardly.

"Very nice," Michael said flatly. "Go finish your preparations. I must make one more visit before we depart."

"Ah, the Lady Julia," Sharona said. "I should like to meet her."

"Well, this is a private meeting."

"I can be your chaperone!"

"Not required. Now move along and tease somebody else."

Michael never found out if that would banish Sharona, for at that moment the door opened and Julia appeared, dressed in a fine gold-colored cinched-waist gown that had lace trimmings at the neck and sleeves. Her brown hair was arranged in braids that covered her shoulders and she wore pale makeup.

Michael bowed quickly. "Julia, I-"

"My, that is quite a dress!" Sharona said.

"You may go, Sharona," Michael said, in a polite tone that was obviously forced.

"Ladies like when you compliment their clothes, you know."

Julia smiled at Sharona, then looked her up and down. "Yes, well I did not want to look threadbare to receive home a victorious warrior."

"Please go," Michael said softly.

Sharona raised one eyebrow and smirked. She eyed Julia up and down and said, "Michael's a bit sensitive about it, and he shouldn't be, really, as he's a war hero and all, but he's been sacked. See you later, my prince." She bowed low and held the position as she backed down the hallway, letting her black hair hide her face for a few moments.

Michael was gritting his teeth.

"Go home!" he called after her.

She turned her back and put up a hand in response.

Michael turned back to Julia and forced a smile.

"I apologize, she's a mage from my cadre who, well… it's hard to explain."

"Come in and tell me about it," Julia said warmly. She gave a high pitch *wup* as the laces on the back of her dress suddenly snapped, and her breasts adjusted, threatening to spill out of the low neckline of the dress. She quickly covered herself up. "Margo! This dress! Uh… Just a moment, Michael, come in a sit down while we fix this."

Michael tore his eyes away from Julia's chest to catch a glimpse of Sharona walking down the hall, flipping her hair over her shoulder. *Could she have? No…*

"Come in." Michael turned back to see Margo, Julia's attendant, ushering him into a sitting room. He found a comfortable chair and sat down, watching as Margo disappeared behind a privacy screen to help Julia.

"So who was that woman?" Julia said.

"She's a mage, and was very instrumental in our final battle against Ferralla. She's been following me since then. She seems to think I need some sort of protection."

"You haven't sent her away?"

"I've tried to."

"In a gentle way, I assume."

"Yes, but she's rather stubborn," Michael said.

"And rude."

"That's the first I've seen her be out and rude, actually. Mostly she's a nuisance, if a useful one in a pinch."

"Is what she said true?"

"Yes. I…" Michael sighed. "I was avoiding coming and telling you. I was ashamed, I suppose, though I know you wouldn't judge me so."

"Ashamed of what? You're a war hero, she said."

"Yes, well… I broke ranks to enact a maneuver in the battle, which was instrumental in our victory - by my analysis, at least - and was stripped of rank for disobeying orders."

"That's horrible," Julia said, appearing from behind the privacy screen looking prim again. She took a seat beside Michael and laid her hands on his arms. "I know how much your position meant to you. Nobody should expect you to risk it by disobeying orders unless it was absolutely necessary."

"It was. At least…" Michael covered his face with a hand. "At least I thought so at the time."

"You think differently now?"

"Johan explained some other possibilities that had not occurred to me. So I have... had... some doubts as to whether my actions were right."

"If they were right given all the information you had at the time, shouldn't that justify them? I thought that was how military decisions were judged."

Michael nodded. "You're right of course. I think, personally, that had I not acted the way I did General Butler's - your father's - battle plan might have failed." Michael leaned close to her, and suddenly noticed the smell of her perfumed soap. "Ballaco, your father's nemesis, ordered a whole battalion of his troops down a ravine on our northern flank. It would have been terrible for a flanking operation, but it would have separated our reserves and our tired front lines. We would have lost. He only would have done this had he known our forces would push far enough afield that our reserves would be locked well back." Michael looked away from Julia, thoughts racing. "He had to have planned it all, which means he had to know of our plans to begin with. He led the force himself."

"You suspect treachery?" Julia said, almost whispering.

Michael nodded. "It has to be."

"Who?"

"Towler," Michael said. "It has to be him. There were only five us who knew the battle plan ahead of time. Four of us are directly or indirectly tied to my household. Only Towler isn't. He's the only one, as a man ignoble, and a foreigner, who has any reason to betray us. He threw Sharona out of the army because she was part of the force that killed Ballaco."

"Ballaco is dead?"

Michael smiled for a moment. "Yes, by my hand."

Julia's face creased in sadness. "Oh Michael, you deserve a medal. I will talk to Johan about it. Are you sure it is Towler?"

"No, but that is why I must attend these negotiations with the Queen of Ferralla. I must find out and nail him down before he squirms away."

"I see. Well, I will pray to Verbus for your safety. Is there anything I can do to assist?"

"Keep your ears open," Michael said. "I don't know if this is a conspiracy or not." He reached into his jacket and withdrew the letter. "I didn't come to discuss conspiracies with you, though. I came to deliver this."

Julia smiled and took the letter from him. She broke the seal and spread out the scroll as she walked over to her desk.

"What does it say?" Michael said.

"Just letting me know he was safe, and what happened at the battle. He's concerned for you."

"He has strange ways of showing it."

"He *is* concerned, you know," Julia said looking up.

"I didn't mean that sarcastically."

Julia nodded. "Do you have time for me to write a return letter?"

"Yes, of course."

"Good. Make sure you tell him about your thoughts, and I will mention them myself as well."

"I don't see how I could avoid telling him," Michael said.

Michael waited as she wrote the letter, watching her hands working the pen and wondering… she looked up at him and smiled, and he stared at his boots. When she had finished, she sealed it with wax. Michael stood up as she walked back to him.

"Here," she said, and put a hand lightly on his arm. He took the letter and tucked it into his jacket pocket. She ran her fingers down to his hands and held them. "Please take care of yourself, Michael." She ran her thumbs over his knuckles and gazed up at him.

"I will," Michael said. "I can't stay longer."

He cleared his throat, released her hands and walked to the door.

"Don't take too many risks," she said again.

Michael nodded to her and walked out the door.

*

"Are we even now?" Michael said. He had let Calot follow the road at his own leisure, but the beast had chosen to walk beside Rabble-Rouser, Sharona's claimed destrier. Neither of them had spoken to each other yet. The morning had worn on, a light grey rain falling on the traveling cloaks that obscured the face of each, making the silence tolerable for longer than Michael had expected.

"Even? You're still quite a bit taller than me, actually," Sharona said at length, her face hidden in the heavy wool of her cloak and her head unturned. "The extra hand on Rabble-Rouser isn't enough, I'm afraid."

Michael shook his head. "Why do I bother?"

"That's a question you ought to answer to yourself, though if you want the answer I prefer for you to have, I suppose I can give it to you."

"I'm saying I no longer owe you anything, after what you did with Julia," Michael said with clenched teeth.

"All I did was tell her the truth, and support my commander in his plan."

"You were exceedingly rude to her!"

"She was rude to me."

"How, exactly?"

Sharona turned to look at him, and her eyes were cold. "The way she looked at me. *Appraisingly.*"

"That's not rude. She didn't do anything to you. She didn't even say anything-"

"She thought rudely, then."

Michael grumbled. "Look. We're even. I owe you nothing now, alright? That's all."

"Was I ever indebted to you?" Sharona said.

"No, I-" Michael hesitated. "I was indebted to you - only in a small way, mind you - for your actions in battle."

"You were never indebted to me. Suppose I did something of value, such as knock over a line of sticks. Who benefited, exactly? Surely not you. Or I. Well, I did, in a way. It's nice talking to a prince, even an exceedingly stubborn one."

"The kingdom benefited."

"I suppose. Of course, the battle might have been won anyway."

"Perhaps."

"Then who benefited? I say it was the companies of men we saved. They're the ones indebted to me, but of course, they also saved me by… standing there. With their shields?"

"Holding the line, or the shield wall, as we say," Michael said. "You really did skip a bit of training, didn't you?"

"The captain. Sorry, I don't remember his name-"

"Lucido would have been your captain, under my father's legion in Calasora."

Sharona shrugged. "He said I was needed at the front lines immediately. That my talent was too high to bother putting me through a basic military education."

"That says something," Michael said. "Lucido has judged many a mage in his time. You must be talented indeed."

"I know what I know, and that's it."

"Same for all of us."

"Not quite for a mage. Do you know much about magic?"

"Honestly, no, other than I can send a mage to make things burn and burst apart. They're damn useful."

Sharona chuckled slightly. "You *are* like your brother a little bit. Not very much, though, which is good. Since you know nothing of magic, it is good you have me to protect you."

Michael was silent for a moment.

"Not going to deny it this time? Good," Sharona said.

"I hear tell that Queen Alanrae is a sorceress herself," Michael said.

"I hear that too. You expect me to protect you from her?"

"I don't know. You know about magic. Perhaps you can protect me, or my family, in the absence of Towler."

"I will protect you, Michael."

"What about my brother and father?"

"I am powerful, according to some, but even I cannot be in three places at once."

"And yet you seem to hold dominion over more than one object at once."

"Ah, so you liked my little trick."

"I appreciate that you can do it," Michael said.

"It's a start. Women love praise, you know. You should listen to Guissali more often."

*

The next day, the rain increased, gradually getting worse as the day wore on, darker and filled with lightning. Sometime around sunset, Michael admitted defeat and had his retinue of servants begin making camp amid a cluster of old, high hardwoods that, if they did not keep much rain off of them, at least broke the incessant wind. Guissali, who had jumped at the opportunity to act as Michael's retainer for the journey, ordered the servants about vigorously, clapping his hands if he felt they were too slow in their purpose.

"There's a town and an inn not so further up the road," Sharona said. "If I remember our journey to the capital."

"We need to take a fork before we reach Gabora Minor," Michael said. "Since we are taking the swiftest route to Forgoroto, not retracing the armies steps into the hinterlands of Ferralla. With luck, we will be there in time."

"There's no such thing as luck," Sharona said.

"Then with the blessings of the gods."

Sharona smiled a little smile and nodded. She led Rabble-Rouser over to a nearby tree and kneeled down. Michael watched her light a few twigs on fire with a flick of her finger, then stack some more wood on it.

"Dead handy, that is, sire," said a nearby servant.

"It is," Michael said, watching her. She began to stack sticks up, not on the fire, but beside it, then tied them together. With a little tug, she bent the sticks and the oak above began to creak. Leaves shook in the wind as the branches bent over her, making a small roof.

"What's your name?" the prince said, grabbing the wrist of the servant as he moved to walk away. "I don't know you."

"Langelo, sire," the young man said, bowing while allowing the prince to handle his wrist. "I normally muck the stables, sire, but I was asked-"

"Langelo. I want you to provide a good meal for my mage friend. And have a tent pitched for her. Her little house might be impressive, but it won't keep this water out."

Michael walked over to Sharona, who sat beside the fire, gazing at it with eyes that were near glazed. Without speaking, he took a twig and put it in the fire. It sputtered for a moment as the water on it boiled off, then a small flame leapt up on it. Michael used it to light his pipe, a long-stemmed briarwood affair of striking artistry, which he had packed in the morning but neglected smoking due to the rain.

"I'm having a tent set up for you, and some dinner prepared," Michael said between draws.

"Thank you. I shan't need the tent," Sharona said.

"This roof is impressive, I will admit, but a tree cannot provide the shelter of a properly oiled and waxed piece of canvas, even if you have enchanted it so."

"With the fire, I think I'll be fine."

"Allow me to extend my grace."

"No."

"Then indulge me."

Sharona laughed softly and finally looked up at Michael. "Fine."

Michael blew a smoke ring over the little fire, and watched it fly up into the branches on the draft. "So, how does magic work? How do you do it?"

"Those are two different questions."

"Very well, the first."

Sharona said, "I wish I brought my pipe. I lost it a long time ago."

"It's not usually considered polite for women to smoke."

Sharona shrugged. "Not so where I'm from. In the Dobo Wold, no such pleasure is made exclusive to one sex or the other."

Michael smiled. "Well, I have an extra in my bag. Shall I fetch it for you?"

"That's alright," Sharona said. "You're already sitting here."

"Yes. Now about magic…" Michael raised his eyebrows.

"Magic is when you bring a part of the eternal into the mundane. Here, when we are in this part of the world," she gestured around her, "within the mundane, the spiritual world, which is the world of real things, is far away. If you are in touch with the eternal dream, as some of us are, those parts of the dream which you truly know and understand may be brought here, just as a man brings the memory of his dream into the waking world."

Michael laughed softly and puffed his pipe. "I can't say I really understand."

"You can't until you do. That's the problem. Mages that are strong, or weak, are so because of how well they dream when they are awake. Or maybe, how well they remember the dream. Did I tell you I've been there? To the eternal dream?"

"You said you'd been to the Fay Lands, if they exist."

"They exist more and less than the rest of the world."

"That doesn't make any sense."

"It does, but like you said, you don't understand."

"True."

"Most mages have never been there. It's dangerous because you can forget who you are in the waking world, and be lost inside it forever."

"You said it made you go mad," Michael said. "Or rather, some people thought it had made you mad."

"I did not return unchanged."

"So how do you do magic? Or maybe, how do you do so many different things? I only ever see other mages blasting things apart or lighting things on fire."

"That's because most mages are quite weak with their connections to the world of true things. Most mages spend years studying a single concept with many different incantations before they are able to reliably call upon that thing. I had the idea to go to the Fay and find the original dreams myself. Alas, I found them, but did not fully understand them."

"But I have seen you do much magic."

Sharona nodded. "The fire is the easiest. Every mage understands fire, because it is so chaotic and yet simple. It always looks different, instant to instant, but is always itself. Consuming fuel, giving heat and light. I have a terrible time trying to understand the true nature of concepts past fire and other simple things." She looked up. "Once, mages could control the weather. I wouldn't mind that, but…" She sighed.

"How did you bend these tree-limbs, then?"

"Well, I'm bad at understanding true things, but I'm very good at making comparisons and finding categories. I have found that if I have two objects and understand deeply their sameness, I can manipulate one through the other. A stick is the same as a tree limb, for example. The only difference is what they are attached to."

"I've never seen that talent before," Michael said.

Sharona put on a half smirk and stared at the fire again. "Nor are you likely to again. It is a unique gift, and, like I said, most mages are rubbish."

"Well, I'm glad to have your talents here, as I was glad to have them in my legion."

Sharona sighed.

"What?" Michael said. "What's that about?"

She looked up at him again, her eyes sad. "I just…" She paused for a moment more, and her face went back to its placid slight smile. "I was thinking about the queen of Ferralla, Alanrae. She has a terrible reputation as a mage. And by that I mean she is very powerful. Very strong. Just wondering what I can do against her. Probably nothing. That's what the sigh was about."

Michael watched her for a moment, imagining the fleeting look of sadness that had been seemingly washed away. "Well, I don't think we need engage her directly, merely defeat her plan."

"Of course," Sharona said. "And you won't be getting rid of me by bringing up Alanrae, you know. I intend to do…" She hesitated and bit her lip, "to protect you."

Michael forced a smile. "Let me see if I can get us some food."

"If the servants don't bring it first."

"Yes, of course," Michael said, and sat back down. He tapped on his boot for a few moments, then said, "Wait, I saw you make those bandits keel over in pain with bee stings."

Sharona's eyes lit up and her face regained her usual smirk. "I understand the pain of bee stings very well, when I can remember them, which isn't always, oddly, but when I *can* remember them, I can put them on, sometimes, a few people at a time."

"So you've been attacked by a swarm of bees?"

"Oh yes, they stung me horribly as a girl. They scarred me very badly, and when I think of the scars, I can feel the pain. You can see it's a weapon I prefer not to use."

"I see no scars," Michael said. "You look perfectly comely to me."

"Thank you," Sharona said without inflection.

V: FERRALLA

The sun was shining brightly on the plain as Michael, Sharona, and the handful of servants and guards they had brought worked their way slowly down from the rocky pass separating Ferralla and Artalland. The sparse dry oaks on the leeward side of the mountain were little shelter from the sun, and soon everyone in the party was loosening collars and removing jackets to cool off.

Langelo came riding awkwardly toward them from up the road, his horse (borrowed from one of Michael's retainers, who slept happily in the wagon) second-guessing his commands and turning this way and that in its gait.

"Sire! There is a detachment of soldiers up ahead. Ferrallese soldiers," Langelo said, the horse drifting past them and rearing its head against the tight hold on the reins.

"I see," Michael said, reaching out a hand to calm the snorting destrier upon which Langelo was perched. "How large a group?"

"Fifty, maybe sixty men."

"We need not be afraid, my lord," said Guissali. "You are the victorious prince!"

"Ferralla hasn't surrendered just yet, Gui," Michael said. "These soldiers are obviously stationed here to guard the border. Insurgency is a problem in times of war, and more so as a conflict resolves, and remember that we are not far from Structania, who has never forgiven Ferralla for the rift during the old war. I predict they will be unwilling to just let us pass on. Hold up here."

"What do you have in mind, my lord?" Guissali said. "Shall we work our way around, or have your mage give them a good fright?"

"I should have anticipated this," Michael said. "Trying to avoid them may prove difficult. If they are guarding the border here, they probably will have scouts around these parts for such an occurrence. It is likely we have already been seen and are being tracked."

"You've become such a pessimist lately," Sharona said. "If they did see us they will think us merchants with our guard. Nobody is wearing anything fancy. We'll just tell them we're out to sell something in Ferralla."

"I guess they might think that," Michael said. "Of course, we carry no goods."

"We could be traveling to buy, not to sell," Sharona said.

"Then they'll want to rob us," Guissali said. "Soldiers without a solid command quickly turn brigand, your highness."

"Well, if you have a better idea, I'd like to hear it," Michael said.

Guissali scratched his chin. "I say we turn around and head back through the hinterlands, in the path of the army. Nobody will bother us on that road."

Michael shook his head. "You don't know that, and we don't have the time. I'd be willing to play dice with what Sharona said... but if they find out who I am, they'll capture me with a mind to ransom me in the upcoming negotiations."

"Well, sounds like it will be on me to do the legwork," Sharona said. "I'll be hard pressed, but-"

"I have another idea," Michael said. "That will put us all at less risk. Langelo, are you a good liar?"

"Sire?" said Langelo.

"Are you a good liar? Can you tell a lie convincingly?"

"He's no noble, I'm sure," Sharona said.

"I think so, sire," said Langelo.

"Good. And are you loyal to a fault?" Michael said.

"To a fault?" Langelo said.

"Sire, *I* am loyal to a fault," Guissali said.

"I know, but you're also a terrible liar, hence why I appreciate you, and also why you have been stuck as a palace retainer for twenty years."

"Sire... I don't understand," Guissali said, his dark face creasing with a deep frown.

"Never change, Gui," Michael said, smiling. He turned back to Langelo. "You're going to deliver a little message for me to the Ferrallese commanding officer."

Langelo rode to the assembly of cavalry flanking the men on the road, who were armored lightly but bore stout shields. They had a number of wagons set up, easily movable to create a quick barricade, but presently they were sitting off on the grassy shoulders of the road. Langelo did his best to hold the great destrier steady, holding up his hand as he rode forward in a symbol of peace.

Several men with crossbows lowered their aim as he approached, at a signal from a knight armored with a coat of plates over tarnished mail. His face was gaunt and creased into a permanent frown over a thin beard of black.

"Who goes there?" said the soldier, his voice high and sharp.

"Messenger, sir," Langelo said, and pointed to a bag at his hip. "Looking to pass through to Ferralla and bear news to the court of Alanrae."

"What news?" The knight said. "Give it to me and I will see it safely sent."

"I was… um, instructed to share it only with the queen's court."

"He's lying, cap'n Philo," said one of the soldiers. "String him up and see what letters he's got, and what coin."

"No! Don't do that!" Langelo said. "I… I'll give the message to you, sir," he nodded to the first knight to speak, "if you will assure me you will send it on properly, and that you are in command, of course. I'm not paid to die."

Philo looked at him with narrowed eyes. "Very well, give me the letter."

"I… I can't sir. It's an oral message, in case I was, erm, intercepted."

The knight frowned and looked to one of the other soldiers.

"Then why the bag?" said Philo.

Langelo coughed and nearly choked. "Vittles and such. I will, uh… share the message with you in private. Yes, private only."

Philo chewed his cheek for a moment and said, "Very well, come to my command tent."

Langelo nodded carefully and dismounted, following the knight past the soldiers and into a small camp. They halted outside a small and shabby canvas tent, just high enough for a man to stand when inside. The knight held back the flap and allowed Langelo to enter. The interior was sparsely furnished and dimly lit by two ports cut into the cloth overhead.

"Well, spit it out, if you don't want to be put on a spit," the knight said, drawing his sword.

Langelo gulped and nodded. "Let me show you…" He reached for a pouch at his belt and felt the tip of the knight's sword touch his shoulder.

"It's not a weapon, my lord," Langelo said, his voice shaking. He took the pouch and held it forward to the knight, opening the top slightly. Inside was the unmistakable glint of gold.

"Where'd you get this?" The knight said, taking the pouch.

"There's more where that came from, if you can hold command of your troops."

"Of course I can hold command. What is your proposal?"

"Nothing substantial. Just move your men off the road and a few miles to the west, where the river runs. You can say you gained information from me regarding an incursion. Once I'm through, you collect another payment at the place I will tell you of."

The knight shook the heavy bag for a moment. "How about I collect the rest right now?"

"I don't have it on me."

"So I'll just wait for you to come back with it."

"I won't be back with it if you don't move your men."

"You know what? I think you're lying. I think you're just going to run off and I'll never get the rest. I have a mind to keep this and have you hanged. At least then I'll be doing my duty to my queen by preventing any spies through."

"Don't you know you've lost the war?" Langelo said. He swallowed hard. He wasn't supposed to say that.

"We'll see. The queen still sits upon the throne and Forgoroto has yet to be breached." The knight smiled. "And now I know you're not Ferrallese as well."

"Fine," Langelo said with a hard swallow. "I'll take you to them."

"To who? Your conspirators?"

"The… My employers. Who have the rest of the money."

"Good. Let's go."

Langelo stuck his hands in his pockets and followed the captain's sword tip toward the flap of the tent. As he lifted the flap, a twig snapped, causing the captain to flinch.

"What the hell is this?" Philo hacked at the empty barrels with his sword, sending them rolling around the back of the empty wagons.

"I… I don't know," Langelo said. He approached the wagon and looked at the empty bed, scratching his head with his bound hands. "This is where I was supposed to come back to meet them."

"What's this?" one of the soldiers said. He held up a strip of paper. "I can't read."

Philo snapped it out of the soldier's hand and read it. "Blast it, it's for this scum here. Says they abandoned the wagons and went round the north side, where the river runs. Run down and have both squads move to cover the river valley. Go."

One of the soldiers saluted. "And what of the prisoner?"

"Leave him to me."

"Aye," the soldier said, and mounted his horse. He shot down the road in a puff of dust.

The captain turned to Langelo. "What are you playing at?"

"Nothing."

The captain walked to the edge of the wagon and kicked Langelo in the head, sending the boy sprawling. Philo leapt down from the wagon and moved to kick Langelo again, but as he wound his leg up he heard a soft crack and collapsed. He was in shock for a few moments, then the pain kicked in with force and he began to scream in agony. Langelo spun up in shock, his eyes wide as he watched Philo writhe on the ground.

The one remaining soldier ran over, drawing his sword, but was hit in the neck with a crossbow bolt that burst the links of his mail coif with ease.

Sharona, Michael, and Guissali stumbled down the hillside from behind a rock. Michael was holding his crossbow, already fitting on the crank he used to span it while in the saddle. Langelo pushed himself up and stared at the thrashing, screaming captain, clawing at his misshapen leg like a beast.

"I'm sorry, Langelo," Sharona said with a huff as they crossed back into the road. "I should have done that sooner. Luckily I've been saving chicken bones."

Michael ran to the captain and kicked him in the head, rolling him over. With a toe, he stilled the man, then bent down and cut the bag of gold from his belt.

"Glad you were able to snap that twig," Michael said, putting the gold in the bag at his hip. He moved to Langelo and began untying his hands.

"Me too," Langelo said. "I don't think I care to be a spy, sir."

"Understood, but I think you did well," Michael said.

"What should we do with the captain, my lord?" Guissali said.

"Let him cry with that broken leg. I have no compassion for greed."

"To his credit," Langelo said, "Philo did try to protect his border."

"He took the gold," Michael said. "That would be enough for me to hang him, were he under my command."

"You're - I saw you once... You're the prince of Artalland," the soldier croaked.

"So I am. Good luck telling that tale."

"Lord," Guissali said. "I cannot allow you to endanger yourself by letting such a man pass on the truth that you are in Ferralla."

Michael took a breath and nodded. "Make it merciful."

"Yes, my prince," Guissali said. He looked at Sharona and said, "My lady, please avert your eyes." Sharona obeyed.

Though he might have been held a lowly retainer due to politics, Guissali was as deadly with a blade as any knight of Artalland could be; with a single swift stroke of his heavy curved blade, he severed the head of the Ferrallese captain, ending his suffering and misdeeds in the world that is.

Langelo, watching the head roll away, suppressed a retch. Michael patted him on the back.

"It's never pleasant, son," he said.

*

"It was necessary," Michael said.

"I didn't say anything," Sharona said. They were riding out past the Ferrallese army encampment, their troops having left it abandoned save for a few cowardly men who refused to bar the way forward as they approached, instead merely asking their business and letting them pass when they saw a match of their numbers in men that bore swords and lances.

"The look on your face said that you didn't care for our dispatching of the captain."

"I don't believe it was the only solution, 'tis true," Sharona said. "I broke his leg so we would not have to kill him. Otherwise, I would have done something to simply kill him quickly."

"If we didn't kill him, the army would have, for bribery and other high crimes. The only other solution would be to take him with us, and we can't spare the thought for an injured man. If anything, we treated him mercifully, for the army would have given him much more pain in the departure."

*

Sharona rode beside Michael along the wide road that cut through the open plains of Ferralla. Farmhouses long gone to ruins dotted the yellow-green landscape around them, along with remnants of stone walls and the occasional fence post. Herds of antelope roamed unmolested between groves of dry oaks and willows near creek beds. Dry grass at the tops of the hills rippled in the high wind.

"How much longer, do you think?" Sharona said.

"By our old catalogues, we will reach the city tomorrow night. We should find some semblance of civilization today, though I think we may find it somewhat diminished."

"What happened here?"

Guissali cleared his throat. "My lady, do not trouble yourself over the details. The people that were here… left."

"I am strong of stomach, if you are thinking of describing a battle, or plague," said Sharona, smiling at the frowning Guissali, bent over on his horse in a sort of bow.

"It was one, then the other," Michael said. "But of a terrible sort. It is considered bad luck to speak of it."

"I told you that there is no such thing as luck," Sharona said.

Michael smiled. "It was during the reign of my grandfather, when the kingdoms of the Divine Strand were poised to once again be united as the once great Empire of the Divine. Pious Patruffi, the king of Verbia by original title, was uniting all the twelve kingdoms, one by one, under the banner of the Golden Sun. The first few kingdoms to fall - Nautalia and Nosterina, if I remember well my books - fell by the white sword, but the other kingdoms, witnessing the might of Verbia and the swiftness with which Pious was reorganizing their militaries in imperial form, soon began to form tentative alliances with one another, which is unheard of in these late times.

"The conquest continued, but mostly via civil machinations. Pious satisfied many by removing the title of emperor from himself and agreeing that it should belong to his daughter. A daughter that would be birthed by the princess of Ferralla, that being the only country whose military might could withstand him without an alliance."

"Why a daughter?" Sharona asked.

"That no king might seek the seat of the empire for himself. The idea of an empress tempted many, for therein seemed to lie the prospect of peace in our wide lands. Even my grandfather Tomas, shrewd and cautious, saw the virtue in it and soon swore fealty to Pious."

"He saw the way the wind was blowing, your highness," Guissali said. "He was never a fool to believe in prophecies and promises. He knew that if Ferralla was under the influence of Pious, we wouldn't stand a chance on the battlefield. Better fealty with conditions than servitude in conquest."

"Guissali has his opinions," Michael said. "Being a great veteran, he sees it partly as it was. There was no way we could resist without

73

DAVID VAN DYKE STEWART

our alliance with Ferralla. But," Michael raised a gloved finger, "these things did not come to pass. The princess of Ferralla, the mother of queen Alanrae, usurped her father and claimed the monarchy for herself. In truth of course the coup had been staged by the Artallan spymasters. Adonala was the name of the princess, and her coup was swift and total, supported by most of the land's lords. The king was forced into exile.

"She nullified the arranged marriage with Pious, who was more than twenty years her senior, and the great war began."

"This plain held a great battle," Guissali said. "The greatest that has been fought in the Fourth Dominion. It was here that Pious revealed a bit of who he really was - an apostate and a sorcerer. He used... forbidden magic."

Sharona raised an eyebrow to Guissali, who chewed his lip.

"He raised the dead," Michael said. "A forbidden act, even among mages, or so I am told. A contagion was spread, and men fell. They rose again as undead thrall."

"That is ancient magic," Sharona said. "I presume he was stopped?"

"Yes," Michael said. "The church removed its blessing. The clerics fled. My grandfather betrayed his oath and turned on Pious. With Ferralla and Artalland working together, Pious was stalled, even as the ranks of the dead grew. What happened after is… uncertain."

"It was a dragon," Guissali said. "A dragon brought the men of the north down and slew Pious."

"It was not a dragon," Michael said.

"Not to contradict you, your highness, but there were many there who saw it. My own sire, for one."

Michael shrugged. "Well, there *was* a cadre of sorcerers who came from the north, mostly a mix of elves and men of the petty kingdoms. Nobody was sure of who assembled them, but they broke the stalemate and gave the dead back to the peace of the earth. Pious was killed by my grandfather in the final fight, but Tomas was struck dead as soon as his sword fell, a consequence of his betrayal and the magic that Pious had laid on him when he swore fealty."

"That's where Towler's from," Guissali said. "He came down at the end of the war and just ended up sticking around, helping the young king do everything important."

"How did you go from being allies to enemies?" Sharona asked.

"Politics," Michael said. "Ferralla failed to honor agreements made in the wake of that conflict, which, if I am to be honest, could not be met anyway."

"What about your father's aims?" Sharona said. "Did he not wish conquest?"

"He *does* desire conquest. He is not faithful Tomas, after all. However, one cannot propose a campaign of conquest in the high court of Artalland, for it is now considered exceedingly distasteful. You have to cook up other reasons for a war to fund the damn thing, and then act like conquest is a happy accident when you pass out new fiefdoms to your power base.

"Now that we are at last successful in this war, these lands can be re-settled by Artallan people, the fields resown and renewed."

"If anyone will come," Guissali said.

*

They stayed in a town called Lore that night, under the story that they were merchants traveling to Forgoroto, though the mood in the town was sombre and nobody, not even the sheriff, seemed to care about their story. Many of the houses stood dark and shut. Whether they were abandoned for a long or a short while, they could not say, for the occupied houses looked as shambled as those left empty.

The next day brought them within sight of Forgoroto, which was built upon a defensible hill of rock, its proud gates of iron shut and guarded, its banners bearing a bright red hammer flying proudly in the winds of the plains. Before it and around the walls stood en-camped the great first army of Artalland with its three legions. Michael's legion now flew the green banner of Butler's command, a sign that he had truly been excised from the force he had spent the last few years training and deploying in war to great effect. He gritted his teeth as he gazed.

Michael watched the fires of the night, in both city and the army camp, being lit from where he had set up with his own party, on a tree-clad hill a mile or two away. A fenced area within the camp held what Michael knew to be the remaining prisoners of war from the last battle, a bargaining chip to proceed a possible siege, though Michael thought from the size of the enclosure a good portion of the Ferrallese army had managed to flee back to Forgoroto and add to its final defense, or else been turned loose while disarmed as part of the conditions of surrender, which Michael knew nothing of.

Michael stood as a horseman approached. The man atop waved a banner on a lance that could just be discerned to be blue in the failing light.

"Angelico!" Michael said, laughing as his friend rode forth. "I thought you'd have been discharged for sure!"

Angelico slowed and dismounted. "Evening sir. I *was* discharged actually, along with the sergeant major. Butler gave me a new commission before I could pack up and leave camp. He offered to reinstate Gadero, even demanded it, but the old sot said he'd as soon be hung a deserter as work a day past when his proper retirement ought to begin." Angelico laughed. "Butler wanted *you* back, too, but you left so quickly. You might yet get your commission back, actually. I can just talk to Butler for you; tell him you are here."

Michael was silent for a moment, mulling it over in his head.

"I don't think so, just yet at least," he said. "I didn't come here to try to get my position back. I came here because I believe there is a traitor somewhere in high command."

"What?" Angelico said. "Come off it."

"Have you spent much time thinking about the battle?"

"Well, yes of course, sir. I've been thinking about how damn lucky I was you showed up."

"The luck was Palsay seeing the approach of the Ferrallese division, if there *was* any luck. Have you thought about why the enemy sent that many men down that corridor, away from the field?"

"Trying to flank us."

"I forget you weren't in the war council," Michael said. He scratched his chin nervously. "I foiled a plan to make us lose that battle. Someone in the council sent a message to Ballaco, and he acted on it. I believe it is Towler, but I cannot prove it yet."

"The mage? Why him?"

"He's the only one that had anything to gain."

"Maybe he sent a message using magic, eh?"

"Maybe, maybe not. A good spy could have gotten a message out without much difficulty. We like to pretend we have good security, but if you spend a little time at the top of command and you know that security always has lots of flaws. Anyway, I need your help to corner Towler before he can try to do anything else."

"What do you think he'll do?"

Michael put his palms up. "I really don't know, partly because I don't know what's going on here. My guess is that he'll do something to push this into a proper siege and then sabotage our efforts."

Angelico looked off to the camp with a puzzled look on his face. "Why not just kill the king? He's around him all the time."

"I don't know, but I presume if that is what he intended he would have already done that."

"Then it seems likely to me to be someone other than Towler. Somebody else lower down the command chain without access to the king."

"Or mayhap he feels the need to escape. It would be easy to do in a battle rout."

"True, true. Or in a siege turned into open battle."

Michael snapped his fingers. "What if he's attending the negotiations with the king?"

"It would be an opportunity to kill your father, whilst everyone in the room is disarmed. He could run away with the Ferrallese, too."

Michael nodded. "We've got to keep him away from the king in that contingency. When are the negotiations taking place?"

"Tomorrow at sundown."

"That's not much time. Is there some way to keep him occupied and away from the meeting?"

"I'll try to think of something. Maybe we could start a fire or let the horses out. An event that would force him to attend to the immediate danger and ignore the council, or risk being outed."

Michael thought for a moment. "I'll present myself tomorrow. My father and brother may accept me into the council as a member of the royal family."

"What are you going to do against a mage?"

"I have my own mage. She's very clever. She was with us in the battle."

"I think I remember her. Sharona? Your brother sent her home quite abruptly. She didn't seem to care, though. Actually, she seemed a bit happy about it."

"My brother sent her on?"

"Yes. It was father who sacked the rest of us. But the prince wanted that woman out of camp immediately for some reason."

Michael frowned. "She *can* be a bit much. Personality-wise, I mean. But she's very talented and a sore asset to be lost to the military."

Angelico shrugged. "That's not my area of expertise - magic."

Michael smiled. "I've learned a bit. Do you have any men you can trust?"

"Of course. Palsay can always be relied upon, as can Doboro. And you've earned a great amount of goodwill yourself. There's plenty of men in the legion who would follow you to Niflheim and back after what you did in the last battle."

"What are they calling that battle anyway?"

"The men are calling it Ballaco's End."

"Good name," Michael said, smiling.

*

Michael startled awake and reached for his sword before realizing the face above him in the dim lantern light was Langelo.

"What is it?" Michael croaked.

"Your Highness, I've seen a man go over the wall."

"What are you talking about?"

"I was keeping watch on our camp. The big army camp, I mean. I saw a man go up to the city wall and over it."

"He climbed the wall, or had a ladder let down?" Michael said, sitting up and rubbing his eyes.

"Neither, Highness. He sort of… floated up."

"Magic?" Michael said, looking around the tent, confused.

"Can't think of anything else."

"It's Towler. We need to watch and see if he comes back down."

"I'm on it," Langelo said.

Langelo came stumbling back into camp as Guissali and Michael were eating a sparse breakfast of eggs and bread.

"Never a sign all night, your highness," he said breathily.

Michael frowned. "We'll have to do better today. Where is Sharona?" Michael added absentmindedly.

"Sleeping still," Guissali said. He shoveled some eggs onto a plate and handed them to Langelo. "I was thinking, your highness. Why not just do Towler in? You're a good shot. I'll put you in the back of the wagon, cover you with hay. I could get you real close to the camp, too. You could just pop a bolt into the mage, and our problem would be solved."

Michael stopped eating for a moment. "I've thought of that, too. But that would be death for all of you, for conspiracy in the assassination of the head of the mage corps."

"But no execution for you. Royal blood and all."

"No," Michael said. "Out of the question. I'll not accept living while my friends hang. Besides, I want to catch and expose Towler, not simply kill him. I don't want his treason to go unrecognized. And I'm no assassin. I prefer to fight a man face to face, in battle, not shoot from the shadows during a peaceful moment."

The flap to Sharona's tent moved and she emerged, clothed in a wrinkled dress and looking disheveled.

"I had a dream," she said affirmatively before sitting down on a rock by the campfire and dishing food out to herself.

"We all had dreams," Guissali said. "I dreamt I was falling into the ocean, but the ocean was stone instead of water."

"I had a dream I was looking in a mirror, but it wasn't my reflection, it was someone else's," Sharona said. "Someone with a different face who spoke to me with a different voice."

"Does it mean something, though?" Michael said.

"It means I'm afraid," Guissali said. "As if we all aren't."

"It means I'm not seeing well enough," Sharona said sadly. "I don't like feeling uncertain."

Michael laughed. "Nobody does, but uncertainty is manifest this day. Let's make a good show of it. Oh, and here." He handed across a small cloth bag. "I got that from one of Angelico's officers, who've been keeping an eye on our little camp for us."

Sharona undid the bag and withdrew a finely carved pipe of dense, dark wood depicting a simple dragon on the bowl.

"It's real Briarwood from the Northmarch."

"Thank you," Sharona said, her eyes narrowing as she examined it. "I… Thank you."

"There's some tobacco in there as well."

Sharona gave Michael a soft smile, and put the long stem in her teeth.

VI: The Queen and the King

ichael stood beside his horse, putting on his gloves. He wore a colorful doublet of blue and green, a fine set of satin trousers and his riding boots, which, as he had neglected to bring formal shoes, were shined with cooking oil as per Guissali's suggestion. He watched the pavilion tent in front of the gates having its final stakes hammered into the ground. It was as neutral a location as could be managed; just beyond reasonable firing range from the city walls and equally far from the fortifications of the Artalland camp.

"Are you sure you'll be let in?" Sharona said, sitting atop her own horse. The wind blew her hair across her face, and she squinted at the westering sun.

"I'm the prince," Michael said. "And I intend to time my arrival in such a way that my father would not dare try to expel me. Besides, Alanrae is a civilian, it is only fitting there be one on the other side as well." He stuck his foot in the stirrup and mounted his horse.

"Here, take these," Sharona said. She handed Michael a small twig and a light canvas bag, the top tied with twine. "Don't open the bag. It's full of charcoal."

"What is it for? Do you intend for me to draw the scene for you on a piece of paper?"

"If you get in trouble, break the twig. I've linked it with one on my person. I'll then ignite the charcoal in the bag, and we'll try to come rescue you. It should create some smoke and fire - enough to blind everyone in the room."

"Don't bother trying to rescue me," Michael said. "I shan't need it, but even if I do, you shouldn't put yourselves at further risk."

"You would come to the aid of one of your commanders, so we shall come to yours. If it is needed, that is."

Michael chuckled. "I'm more worried for you."

"Don't be."

Towler grunted in frustration as his horse bucked and kicked, turning and pulling on the bridle in a frenzy. He dropped his staff and put two hands to work on the reins, but the beast was in a fit.

"What in Grim's gaze is wrong with you?" he shouted at the beast. "What did you do to my horse?" he yelled to the horsemaster as he was turned about.

The horsemaster, a large mustached man named Gratio, was trying to wave over a few lads to assist the mage as he ran about the horse, trying to see if something had hurt it.

"You two!" he cried as two stable boys finally noticed the commotion. "What did you do to this horse?"

"We fed him and walked him," said one of the stable boys.

"Well get on his other side, damn you, let's check his feet for burs."

It was no use. The horse bucked and whinnied, or cried, or kicked and jumped anytime a hand was laid on him.

"Blast it all!" Towler said. "I'll walk. I'm late as it is. And pray for yourself, Gratio, for I shall not forgive you failing my horse!"

"Just give us a minute now!" Gratio said desperately, shielding his face as if expecting the old man to attack him.

Towler picked up his staff and trotted away, sweating with anger. First, he could not find his staff (it had turned up in a pile of firewood), or his formal shoes (which he never found), then his pants had been ripped (causing great embarrassment), and now he had to walk instead of ride all the way to the pavilion.

"It's a damn conspiracy," he said to himself as he rushed through the tents. He felt his feet suddenly moving under himself, and realized he was slipping on something.

He fell and landed in (he realized after a few confused moments) a pile of fresh manure.

"By the dreamer, the gods, or this dratted queen... something is conspiring against me!" With a howl of rage, he flew off the ground, a magic current of air flinging manure everywhere, pelting the tents and nearby soldiers. He turned and pointed at the manure with his finger, and it burst into flame.

*

"Good work," Angelico whispered to Langelo. They were crouching behind a row of barrels, trying to suppress laughter as they watched the dirty wizard rage at a pile of feces. "How did you manage to scare the horse?"

"It was something Sharona did. Made it sting or itch. She said she was surprised it worked. He's coming!"

Angelico and Langelo pushed on a stock of wood buried beneath the barrels. With a creak, they toppled over, spilling water while rolling toward the wizard. The heard him scream in anger as the barrels bowled him over at the knees.

Crouching, Angelico and Langelo dashed behind a row of tents and lumber, listening to the barrels explode amid the cursing of Towler.

*

"Sir, control your horse!"

"I'm trying," Guissali cried to the knight on the ground nearby. Beneath him, Guissali's horse was bucking and braying, forcing the knights around him to get up from where they sat, dining at the long tables.

With a kick, one of the tables was knocked over, spilling beer and food everywhere. The officers cursed at Guissali and threw bits of food at him. Out of the corner of his eye, Guissali saw Towler approach, positively livid.

"Out of the way!" the mage cried loudly. "Or Grim help me I'll blast you all to pieces!"

The officers, however, did not immediately react. Towler pushed his way past the ring of them to where Guissali spun on his horse. The horse kicked at Towler, who held up his staff to block the attack. With a loud crack the staff broke apart and Towler threw it down.

Guissali spurred his horse forward, kicking up mud and food, and not a moment too soon, for just then Towler had cast a tremendous ball of fire that burst the tipped-over table apart and set all the grass around it to blue flame. Guissali looked back to see the mage stomping and screaming as a few officers tried to corral him.

He rode on into the camp and looked west at the setting sun, a satisfying smile on his dark face.

*

"Watch out!"

Towler looked up from the two officers laid on the ground by his conjured wind to see a fence stake flying toward him. He stepped aside, but also saw the large tent beside him leaning, then toppling. The center post hit him square in the shoulder and knocked him down. The canvas fell over him in smothering pleats.

"Damn you!" he screamed. "Damn you!"

*

The two parties rode toward each other in the wide open space between the great gates of Forgoroto and the Artallan encampment.

The queen of Ferralla carried in her retinue two fully armored knights, each armed with a pair of basket-hilted swords, along with an old, unarmed scribe.

The king of Artalland went with his own scribe, his son (armed in his full battle regalia, though the king was dressed simply), but was without a second bodyguard.

As the two came closer to the assigned meeting place, the king turned his head, for he had heard the sound of shouts from his encampment. Toward the meeting place rode, unmistakable upon the back of his destrier, his younger son, carrying the banner of the realm, rather than his own: A silver viol on a field of black.

"What is he playing at?" Johan said as they rode.

The king sniffed. "He aims to attend this negotiation, in a way I cannot now refuse. He is, after all, the official ruler when the king is at war. Not that I think he's done a damn thing."

"What about minister-"

"That changed when we discharged a royal prince," the king said shortly. "Damn that we couldn't wait just a moment longer for Towler, and we could send him away in the interest of even odds."

"It's not like Towler to miss a meeting like this."

"No, but then..." the king shook his head and pointed back toward the pavilion.

Michael got within distance of them, and Johan shouted, "What are you doing here, Michael?"

"I'm asserting my right as prince to attend a diplomatic function."

"Get out of here and go fetch Towler, you fool boy," Eduardo said. "Hurry, before we begin this meeting!"

"If Towler is not here, that is his own business."

Johan yelled over the wind, "Damnit, Michael, you have no idea what you're doing here!"

"I have every idea," Michael said. "It is you that doesn't understand. But I aim to help you even if you refuse it."

Michael watched the angry faces of his brother and father as he slowed Calot to a trot. He turned his eyes to the Alanrae, the Queen of Ferralla. Even far enough away to miss the details of the woman, he could see that she was beautiful. Her hair, black as night, flowed in waves over her slim shoulders and down her back. The dress she wore exposed both her generous breasts and her small waist, and she rode with grace. As they neared the details of her beauty asserted themselves. Her features were noble and pronounced, though she was young and wore them well. Her prominent nose was thin and shapely, her jawline defined but graceful. Her eyes were a bright blue, visible even in the dusk, and they stared hard right into his own.

He met his father and brother as they paused some ten yards from the queen with the tent for the meeting off to their right. The queen's face was smooth and unreadable, her full lips motionless. Only her hair and her jeweled earrings moved in the breeze. Slowly, she raised her right hand.

The king followed suit, raising his bare right hand. The knights imitated this, as did Michael and Johan. They all moved toward the center.

"Greetings," she said in a loud, clear voice. "These are my cousins, Porthonio and Sortonio. I am Alanrae, queen of Ferralla."

"This is my son, Johan, crown prince of Artalland and High Captain of the First Army," said the king. "I am Eduardo, known as Eduardo the Black, King of Artalland."

"And who is this?" The queen said, turning to Michael.

"I am Michael, Prince of Artalland," Michael said. "A civilian, like you."

"Then we are well met. Let us speak of peace."

The king nodded. They all dismounted and handed their reins to a pair of men, one from each camp, then went into the tent. The interior was dark, save for a pair of lamps hanging down, washing the room in warm light. Below these was a table, which had upon it pens, ink, and a neat stack of paper.

Alanrae and her who two cousins (both of whom had removed their helms, revealing twin faces with dark beards of differing lengths) moved to one side of the table and sat down. Michael followed Johan and their father to the other side, then sat as well.

The queen, whose face was solemn and dark, suddenly smiled at Johan. It lasted but a brief moment, but in that gesture was contained a magic almost in itself, as if she had two faces - one the grim blankness of a high mage, the other that of a blushing young woman. Michael watched her cautiously and reached into his pocket to feel Sharona's twig.

For a tense few moments, the two sides of the table merely stared at one another. Slowly, Alanrae drew out a piece of paper and took a pen, which she laid down carefully.

"Our demands," King Eduardo said, his dark voice without inflection, "Are these." He watched as Alanrae picked up a pen and dipped it in an inkwell. "The rest of the debt owed from Ferralla to Artalland, paid in full from the royal treasury. This amounts to three-thousand, two-hundred, and fifty-two aurels, as of last week, interest included. Next, we demand reparations for the cost of the war, in the minimum amount of one-thousand, three-hundred, and thirty-six aurels, to be collected from the royal treasury or writ with interest to be paid in no more than five years' time. Next, we demand, as an assurity of peace between our kingdoms, the battle plain of Pious's Fall, to be settled peacefully by Artalland. By these terms do you surrender to peace."

Alanrae continued writing on the paper, and was quiet for a moment. "If I refuse?"

"Then we will sack the city and replace you on the throne with a vassal of the Artalland crown."

Alanrae nodded without emotion. She looked up and cast her bright-eyed gaze upon each of them in turn. Again, she smiled momentarily. "Let us examine each demand. First, the debt you proclaim we owe you was agreed upon by men long dead, and was for armaments and armor that were returned at war's end, along with supplies that were used by an ally during war. We have paid the portion we actually owe, and refuse to pay a penny more."

"Armaments are no use during peace."

"Then why did your father have them on hand, I wonder?" Alanrae said. "Now let me continue the other points. For the cost of the war, it was a war of aggression by Artalland against a peaceful Ferralla, and we are normally allies. Nor is the campaign actually complete, as my kingdom remains unconquered, and will always remain unconquered. You may have defeated Ballaco, but his army was but one of the armies of Ferralla, and though we are less in number than in the days of the great war, our might is still beyond even your formidable force. Have you not wondered why your advance to the city was unopposed?"

She held up a hand to silence the king and, oddly, he shut his mouth.

"Lastly, the battle plain where so many of our kin fought and died is considered cursed by most of my people. The entirety of this we offer to service any and all disputes between our people. If your men will settle it, that is their prerogative."

Michael watched his father carefully.

"Peace need not be bitterly bought," the king said. "We offer this: the plain of Pious's Fall, the Hills of Norboro south of the Ronta River, and your eastern border will move to the Rotunda River. All these lands are to be settled by Artalland."

"You would seek to diminish Ferralla by claiming its farmland, not understanding it's true strength, but so be it. However I shall, with the uncertainty of Structania on my border, need some assurity of peace between us."

"And what shall that assurity be?" the king said.

"I will have two members of your household come to Forgoroto and live here as bond of our agreement, one male and one female.

One shall be my consort, and the other shall wed Porthonio. In this way, should you wage war again, it shall be against your own blood and your own bones."

"There are no immediate female members of my family."

"Then one male shall suffice." Her eyes wandered over Johan.

The king frowned and looked first to Johan, then to Michael.

"Johan is engaged," Michael said, watching the queen.

The king turned his head and shushed Michael.

"Engagements are not marriages," Alanrae said. "Consider that the price of peace need not be bought with bitter gold or blood, but with bliss."

She then slid over the piece of paper upon which she had been writing, and there was on it already a contract drafted up, with the ceded lands and the bond of one man of the king's house to marry her as consort.

"If we do this, the ransomed man must lose all his rights to the throne of Artalland," the king said. "Agreed?"

"Of course," Alanrae said. "I seek a bond of family, not an empire."

"We shall consider this offer, as should you, and we will finalize any agreements tomorrow," the king said.

"I look forward to it," Alanrae said, and stood. She held forth a hand, and the king shook it. Johan kissed it, and Michael followed suit before they all three shook hands in turn with the cousins.

"Proof even a fool can do something right," King Eduardo said as they trotted back to camp. "Your outburst might have put a seal on this ceding of territory."

"What?" Michael said. "You're not seriously considering having Johan marry that woman, are you?"

The king chuckled. "He would, if I said so, for I am his king, and we would still gain a kingdom. As consort he would have the real power anyway, being a man and a military leader." He looked to Johan. "Sounds interesting, eh?"

"Most definitely."

"What about Julia?" Michael said.

"Michael," Johan said merrily. "Julia and her father would understand. There would still be one prince to marry her to anyway!"

"What?" Michael said. Again he felt his face prickle with sweat.

"I think he's gone deaf, father," Johan said with a chuckle.

"Good. Maybe he'll go mute as well," the king said. "I'm kidding, my boy. This is a good lesson in negotiation, which you must learn, if you can keep yourself under control enough to learn it. By letting the queen know, accidentally, I might add, that Johan was engaged, we enhanced his value. We can make a show of letting him go, demand some more territory or gold, and we either get more than we originally thought possible, or we persuade her to marry you instead, since you're cheaper."

"Marry me?"

"I think it would be great for you, actually," Johan said. "She would lay that temper of yours low."

"Oh, I *do* look forward to tomorrow," the king said. "Shall I arrange a meeting with the queen, just for you, Johan?"

"Not a bad idea," Johan said. "Yes, let's do it. We can have Michael unexpectedly drop in."

"I won't do it," Michael said.

"I am your king and you will obey me," the king said. They turned as they got closer to the camp, toward where the king's tent stood. "Where is that layabout Towler? We were lucky that we didn't need him."

"You were lucky he wasn't there," Michael said. "I have reason to believe he is a traitor, and betrayed us at the last battle."

"Not this foolishness," Johan said. "First I hear it from your officers after you left - I had to discharge fully half of those in command - and now *you're* repeating it. There is no traitor in our house."

"Did you have something to do with Towler not showing up?" the king said. "Did you?"

"No," Michael said. "I came to... to deal with him if he did show up."

"I say again we were lucky," Johan said. "Alanrae dealt in real faith."

"I don't understand," Michael said.

DAVID VAN DYKE STEWART

"Of course not," said the king. "Alanrae is a mage, or have you not heard? We needed Towler there in case she tried to burn us to bits. He would have countered it and protected us. And he's no traitor. I trust him with my life. In fact, I have."

"It is good that you do not have to," Michael said.

"Enough," Eduardo said. "Now head back to your own station. You're a civilian and I don't want you fraternizing with my army."

*

"I'd say Towler was positively jinxed, if we hadn't been the ones jinxing him," Guissali said, stirring the pot of stew over the magical blue fire. "He must have burned down half the camp in a fit of rage."

Michael blew out a smoke ring as he reclined against his saddle. "Well, the negotiations went well enough, but of course with the traitor absent, and no opportunity to expose the treason, my father is as confident as ever in the stalwart loyalty of his mage-general."

"Well, that's to be expected," Angelico said. He was sitting on a rock near the fire, running a whetstone along his spear blade, trying to catch it in the firelight. "At least until we can actually present evidence."

"The battle ought to have been evidence enough," Palsay said. He sat cross-legged beside Doboro. "But he sure did steam when I dropped that tent on him."

"Your father likely wants something more concrete than circumstantial evidence, sir," Angelico said. "If we could find a letter, or at least a legitimate witness to his treachery, we could make a case."

"Logically, Angelico, it has to be him," Michael said.

"Not everyone acts logically, my lord," Guissali said. "Or have you never seen a man in love?"

"Not you too, Gui," Michael said.

"Just trying to provide adequate counsel in addition to a hot meal, my lord," Guissali said.

"What think you, Sharona?" Michael said. "You've been quiet over there."

Sharona's back was to the fire, her eyes on the city. She smoked slowly the pipe Michael had given her. "I don't think out loud, unlike some people."

"Come on," Michael said.

"I shouldn't have left your side," she said, standing up and brushing herself off. She came and plopped down by the fire. "I should have thought about Alanrae being a mage. Had I been with you, I could have disrupted her magic."

"She didn't use any magic," Michael said.

"Are you sure? There are many kinds of magic, Michael, and not all of them are visible and apparent to an untrained observer. She could have turned your water to poison, or..."

"But she didn't do that," Michael said.

"Or caused you to go mad, or see things that weren't there. I almost failed my purpose with my..."

"With what?"

"By doing what you wanted me to do, rather than what you needed me to do," Sharona said with a sigh.

"That's a woman speaking if I've ever heard one," Guissali said with a chuckle. "And sire, don't you go thinking that's always a bad thing. If my wife had baked me pies and cakes, like I'd wanted, why, I'd be too fat to breathe now."

"Instead of merely too fat to fight?" Angelico said, winking at Guissali.

"You want a go, pretty boy?" Guissali said. "Yours wouldn't be the first face I've rearranged."

"Easy," Angelico said. "I was just teasing you."

"I know. Otherwise, I'd have already stomped you into the ground," Guissali said, dishing out some of the stew into a bowl and handing it to Sharona.

"You serving her instead of the prince first? No wonder you're still stuck on guard duty," Doboro said gruffly.

"Ladies always get served first, you cur," Guissali said. He dished out another bowl and handed it to Michael.

"Finally, someone with some sense of manners," Sharona said.

"Manners?" Angelico said, sitting up. "He called Doboro a cur and threatened to stomp my face in."

"Well, he didn't stomp your face in, did he? And you deserved it, calling him fat."

Angelico waved his hand in front of his face, as if shooing a fly. "So sir, what were the results of the negotiations so far?"

"They proceeded extremely quickly," Michael said. "Almost as if the deal was already worked out ahead of time. In fact, the queen wrote the details down of the final deal we arrived at while my father was still making his first set of demands."

"And you doubt magic was at play?" Sharona said.

"I'm sure it was just experienced political playing," Michael said. "We demanded loads of gold. They didn't have loads of gold, hence why their debt to us hasn't been serviced, so Artalland gets some territory instead. The odd thing, though…" Michael took a puff of his pipe and shook his head. "Probably nothing."

"What?" Angelico said.

Michael cocked his head. "She demanded as a peace assurance a spouse from our household for her and one for her cousin."

"Really?" Angelico said. "Odd."

"That's not odd. Been done loads of times," Guissali said. "King wins a war and gets the princess for his wife or his son's wife. That way you conquer the kingdom, in a way, through blood. Most of the royal families of the Divine strand are quite related at this point."

"Yes, but have you heard of the losing side getting a *man* as a spouse?" Michael said.

Guissali chuckled. "Well, they *have* got a queen. Natural to reverse the roles, I suppose."

Angelico snapped his fingers. "Wait, did they mean the royal household proper, not just an extended relation? Are they going to marry you off, sir?"

"Possibly," Michael said. "The queen seemed much more interested in Johan, to be honest. But he's already engaged to Lady Julia."

"Engagements aren't marriage, sir," Angelico said.

"She said the same thing," Michael said. "I think they'll have a chaperoned meeting, just the two of them, tomorrow."

"That'll be two things to keep Towler away from," Angelico said. He laughed. "Ah, but we might be celebrating a marriage of my esteemed commander to no less than a queen."

"Was she pretty?" Guissali said.

Michael smiled. "She was gorgeous, Gui. Everything a young queen ought to be, and more. The stories don't do her justice."

Angelico laughed. "What happens if your brother marries her? How will that work?"

"I'll become king," Michael said.

"So all and all, the day worked out quite well, eh sir?" Angelico said.

"Yes, but tomorrow will reveal the finality of that," Michael said. He looked around. "Where did Sharona go?"

"Must have gone off to relieve young Langelo," Guissali said. "Funny after that talk about not leaving you be."

"Let's enjoy it," Angelico said. "I appreciate her skills, but... ah, you understand, don't you sir?"

Michael frowned for a moment, thinking of what the mage had said. "I do."

"Women be fickle, sire," Guissali said. "Mighty fickle. And you had best mind that one. Her eyes linger my friend, and she's already got your confidence."

"Pah!" Michael said. "Not Sharona."

"Don't say I didn't warn you."

*

"Where did you find this woman?" Michael whispered. He was kneeling in the mud behind a pile of straw, with two mares casually chewing bits of it, obscuring the view of the mess as they walked back and forth. Between the legs of the wandering equines, he caught solid views of a beautiful young woman with bright blonde hair and the pale skin of the Petty Kingdoms as she sat at a table, working with apparent frustration at a puzzlebox. Her dress was perfectly tailored to her slim frame, and had frills of lace and embroidery that spoke to at least a daughter of the bourgeoisie.

"Among the camp followers," Angelico said. "Apparently a favorite of a few officers, though of course none of them seemed to know she was... involved with the others."

"Interesting. She doesn't look much like a prostitute. Far too well-dressed. Far too pretty, and mannered. Innocent, even."

"That's the poison there, sir."

"She's not really selling herself," Sharona said.

"The men seem to think she isn't, but their empty purses disagree," Angelico said.

"Oh, she'll take their money, but she's not selling her body, really," Sharona said flatly. "She sells a man the idea that she finds him interesting and attractive."

They watched as Towler, looking grumpier than the previous day (if that was possible), walked past the young woman and toward the cook. After being delivered a bowl, he turned around and began walking back, blowing the steam off of his meal.

They all watched as a stick appeared from under a table and tripped Towler, sending his meal flying into the air and creating a shower of broth and meat - much of which landed on the young woman. Cursing, Towler rolled over, clearly ready to smite whoever had tripped him, but paused as the blonde woman bent over him, rubbing his head and trying to help him up. Within moments the woman had sat him down on a nearby bench and was working with a towel at drying him off.

"Oy, he's even smiling," Angelico whispered.

"What did I tell you?" Sharona said.

"Let's see if we can sneak off to his tent," Michael said.

Sharona nodded and followed him down the dusty lane.

*

Sharona lit the interior of Towler's tent with a magic fire of blue inside the mage's lamp, which hung from a stand secured by the center pole. It was a messily arranged place, full of strange objects and even a full-size bed, the luxury of which only a prince or a king were likely to also enjoy. Hurriedly, they went through the mage's effects. Letters were scattered all over a portable secretaire, but quick scans indicated nothing odd at play. His inkwell was dry, having been left open, and he had apparently written nothing in some time.

"Over here, a chest," Michael said, pushing some papers off a low wood box to get a closer look. Sharona followed him over.

"I didn't figure he'd have something this mundane," she said. She ran her hands over the top of it, then stood up. "Stand back."

Michael nodded and stood up. With a flick of her hand, the top of the chest burst apart. Flaming bits of wood flew everywhere. Little flames hopped up here and there on letters and carpets. Michael hurriedly tried to stamp these out, while Sharona threw open the chest to examine the contents.

"Dreamer!" She said, coughing. "He's planted a skunk smell in here, or something like it. There's nothing inside but dead beetles."

"Rats," Michael said, waving the smoke from his face.

"No, beetles!" Sharona said in a high voice. "Filthy little crawlies. Luckily, it looks like I killed them all."

"Nevermind. Wait! What is that?"

Sharona froze for a moment and listened. She heard the voice of Towler, laughing along with a female voice, getting louder and nearer.

"What do we do?" Michael said.

"Stand still. Right there," Sharona said. She held her hands forward, her fingers pointing at the ceiling. She closed her eyes and began mumbling something. She turned in a circle. With a rush of air, the bits of battered chest and the letters on top of it flew back into the position they were just in. With a snap, Sharona extinguished the light.

Wide-eyed, Michael pointed to the bed. Sharona nodded and dove under, followed by Michael, who had to squeeze close against her to fit under the bed and keep his boots from sticking out. Just then, the tent flap rose and Towler entered, followed by a woman with a shapely pair of ankles and simple shoes.

"What a whore," Sharona whispered.

"I'll say," Michael whispered back, just as the mattress began to sag.

VII: Knives of Darkness

Sharona pushed herself closer to Michael as the center of the mattress dipped on its tired ropes, threatening to smother her. She pressed her body against his, and Michael could feel her shaking. Their faces were so close that Michael could only see her as a dark blur; her jagged breath filled his ears, vocalizing very slightly in the swift cadence. Michael was pulled out of contemplating this sudden intimacy as the muffled sounds of passion began to pulse through the moving mattress, and he had to give out a whispered groan.

Sharona breathed hotly in Michael's ear, "This is what you intended, was it not?"

"I didn't expect... it to go so quickly," Michael breathed back. He could feel her warmth just past his lips.

"She's apparently very good at her work."

"I don't want to make that judgment."

Sharona pulled one of her hands forward of her face, pointing underneath the secretaire. Michael followed it. Secreted under the folding chair was a small, featureless box, made of a substance that looked like paper.

"A wizard's box," Sharona said.

"Can we reach it?" Michael said.

"If we wait till these two leave."

"That won't happen anytime soon."

Sharona scowled. "Should have looked for something like this earlier. Maybe I can reach-" She scooted herself forward, trying to inch toward the underside of the secretaire.

A dress fell on Sharona, covering her arm and face. Carefully, she slipped back under the bed, leaving the dress where it was. More clothes fell down into the pile. A minute or so later, the sounds above shifted to a more heated rhythm. Two pale, hairy legs dropped in front of Michael's face.

Sharona reached and touched Michael's face, pointing it the opposite way. Michael nodded and they pushed themselves backward, out of the underside of the bed. When their heads exited the dank shadow beneath the mage's bed, the sounds of passion, both sincere and false, became uncomfortably clear. Not daring to sit up, Michael and Sharona crawled to the edge of the tent and felt for a loose place. Michael glanced back and saw the woman's blonde hair shaking as Towler moaned and shouted.

The high mage's face was concealed, and he gave no indication he detected them. Sharona gestured to Michael, and he wriggled over the dirt and edge of the carpet, under the flap, and into the midday sun. Sharona soon appeared beside him, dusting off her dress.

"That was close," Michael said softly. "Let's get out of here." He grabbed her hand and led her away, down a row of tents and away from the hill that housed most of the high commanders.

"Certainly closer than I prefer to be," Sharona said. "To the fornication, I mean."

"Yes, I- I agree," Michael stammered. "What was that little paper box?"

"A wizard's box," Sharona said breathlessly. "It's an elvish device, used to house secrets. It's easily destroyed, and when it breaks, everything inside breaks as well. It's a tricky thing, but I've seen it before."

"You think we would find evidence inside?"

"You assume there is any to find," Sharona said. "It could be full of old love letters. But it also might prove very difficult to break into the box."

"Why? It's made of paper."

"Please listen, Michael. If the box destroyed, so too will its contents. The box is made of paper that Towler has linked to paper within. Just like me breaking a bone. Maybe if we retrieved it, I could break the links within… but maybe not. And if he notices it gone, he may decide it should just burst into flame, wherever it is."

"I'll be damned if it doesn't pique my curiosity," Michael said. "Almost to the point where I'd let Towler follow Johan around, just to get in there and have a peek."

"Is that what he was supposed to be doing?"

"He was supposed to be watching over Johan during his meeting with Queen Alanrae. A bit of a chaperone, I suppose, but it's more likely what my father said, to counter her magic."

"Who is protecting him now?"

Michael scratched at his beard. "I don't know. Probably another mage. But she didn't use any magic last night-"

"You don't know that. We should find them and make sure."

"I'm more concerned with keeping Towler occupied."

Sharona groaned. "He's occupied. The woman will keep him occupied as long as she feels she wants to, I'm sure."

"Well, we did throw plenty of money at her. Maybe you're right. I think Johan and Alanrae were meeting at a grove up by the river, if Angelico heard correctly. We'll need our horses."

*

Sharona pulled up on Rabble-Rouser's reins, stopping him well before Michael allowed his own destrier to slow. Two knights stood a few spans away from each other on the plain. The grove of Willows, a sacred site to the people of Ferralla, stood some fifty yards beyond. The knights, bearing the purple tabard of Johan's legion, each held a crossbow, with a tall lance fitted upright in the saddle.

"What's the meaning of this?" Michael said, pulling up short.

"Nobody is admitted to yonder meeting," said one of the knights, a middle-aged man Michael did not recognize.

"I am a prince of Artalland!" Michael said.

"I am sorry, your highness," said the knight. "But my orders are what they are, and you no longer have command over us."

"It's important."

"Then you can fetch the king, your highness. Until then, we stand for the crown prince."

Michael growled and pulled Calot around, back to where Sharona still sat, patting the neck of her nervous horse.

"Do you really think they'd shoot you?" Sharona said. "You *are* the prince, after all."

"I don't know what to think. Something's afoot."

"I can do something about those men, if you feel it necessary," Sharona said. "Nothing too permanent." She shook a bag hanging at her hip.

Michael took a breath. "No. I'm not going to harm good soldiers simply because they are in my way at the moment. We'll - I'll - go find my father. It's best he does not see you. Sorry."

"Why?" Sharona said, her brow wrinkled.

Michael shook his head sighed.

*

The king looked at himself in the mirror, which had cracked somewhere along the long and bloody road from the Citadel of Artifia. He checked his beard and ran a hand through his hair, then checked the fit of his jacket.

"This is all part of the game and the plan, Michael," he said as a servant polished his boots below him. "You need to pay attention and stop second-guessing me. You will soon be the consort of a queen."

"Then why are you allowing Alanrae to meet with Johan?" Michael said, checking his own boots, which were scuffed and muddy, along with his leggings. The cooking oil that had provided such a good shine the day prior had now collected large amounts of dust.

"To make *you* seem like a compromise, of course."

Michael cracked his knuckles. "You intend to get rid of me. First, my command, now my place as a prince in Artalland."

Eduardo looked over at him, his eyes open wide. He looked back at himself in the mirror. "Yes, that is what I intend."

"Why, father?" Michael said, his voice impassive.

"You leave much to be desired in a king's son."

It was an odd feeling to hear his father speak plainly, a kind of sick relief, for Michael had always felt his father had been disappointed in him and favored Johan.

Michael swallowed and cleared his throat. "What have I done to fail you?"

"Many things," the king said. "But your nature is my primary concern. You are impatient and ambitious. You're an excellent battlefield commander; your men love you, but these things do not make for a ruler. You have never been willing to be patient or to make the trades necessary to allow a fief or kingdom to endure. Frankly, you are a liability at court. You think not at all of your words or what they might mean. Many times I have had to play politics to protect you and our house from your wagging tongue. I imagine you have no idea how many men have wanted to duel you."

"I have always done what is right, and spoken the truth as I see it," Michael said calmly.

"Right is relative, my son. The dictates of the gods are for peasants and their need to be controlled, not for a ruler. The truth… you avoid the truth just as much as the rest of us, but you choose to believe the lie - that is the differences between you and Johan."

The king turned to him, his face calm. "I bring these imperfections to your attention seldom, and perhaps too gently, because of my love for you. I bring them now for the same reason, that you may improve them, but I know now, and this is the truth, that some things are part of the nature of a man, and cannot be changed. Forever he will be pretending, if he acts other than his nature. For this reason, I choose to remove you, to protect our family, but know that I love you, Michael. You will never be king, but I *do* love you."

The king sighed and put his arms on Michael's shoulders. "That is why I will send you not into exile, but into comfort and power, with a beautiful woman. What man could say I do not love my son, given what awaits him?"

"I could," Michael said.

"And there the truth fails you yet again, my son. Now, it is time. Let us create the finality of this war, and celebrate it. Go fetch some clean clothes."

*

"What happened?" Sharona said. "You look pale and disturbed."

Michael didn't meet Sharona's gaze, but stared out at the city of Forgoroto with a frown.

"Michael?" Sharona said, and laid a hand on his arm. He turned back to meet her eyes. "What's wrong?"

"Nothing. The final agreements on settlement will be happening soon. I… I need to clean up."

"What about your brother in the grove?"

"All part of my father's plan, apparently, to make Alanrae desire my brother. He intends for me to marry her, though. He wants... to send me away."

Sharona looked away and rubbed her horse's nose lightly. "If he wants you away, you can simply leave. I'll go with you."

"No," Michael said. "I have a duty to my father and my country, to peace, if it is within grasp. Besides, Alanrae is a queen and a beautiful woman. That will be a good life."

"But will it be your own life?" Sharona said. She looked up at him and he saw that she too was sad.

"Whose else?"

Sharona shook her head and stepped into her saddle. "You should have less muddy clothes. Let's head back."

Michael nodded and mounted Calot.

*

Michael walked to the left of his father between the assembled and armed ranks of the army, determined to match the old man's impassive forward-facing stare. Things were at least laid bare, and whether his subterfuge against Towler had prevented anything or not, there was a truth looming that soon it would no longer be an obligation upon his honor. He would depart the House of Harthino, if things went according to his father's plan. He could not see now how they would not, unless they were thwarted at the last by Towler.

Perhaps I should trust my father more. He has probably considered all of this, he thought to himself, as they walked through the rows of men standing at attention, their armor burnished and shining orange in the fiery sunset. Their faces were clean and hard, their eyes the only thing that moved, watching him and his father and brother walk as kings and princes, arrayed in gold and blue silk.

The meeting place waited beyond the legions, a wide stretch of grass, now missing its tall tent and holding at its center a single wooden table flanked by priests - two from the cult of Artifia, dressed in clean linen, two from the cult of Ferral, wearing black leather. Far on the other side stood the iron gates and the wall of Forgoroto. Before it was arrayed two legions of Ferrallese warriors of various function, with the archer corps lining the parapets of the walls in bright mail.

"I should say something more to each of you," King Eduardo said, as they passed through the last ranks of soldiers: knights and cavalry officers with their lances raised and meeting high above, forming a tunnel of waving flags and painted oak.

"Yes, father?" Johan said, from the King's right-hand side.

"I owe thanks to each of you for this victory. Your command of your soldiers in battle has grown in the campaign, and here we reap what was sown in blood. You too, Michael," the king said, turning to look at his younger son. "This victory is as much yours as anyone's, though I was forced to bring judgment upon you. I regret that I will be giving the best cavalry officer in a generation to my enemies. May you turn your tact to other borders."

"I am still of the House of Harthino," Michael said. "Wherever you send me, you cannot take away my true name. That should be enough to satisfy you, father."

Eduardo nodded. They walked on in silence for a few minutes, the yards from their lines growing until the men looked like an indistinct mass of spears and shields. They approached the table, which was simple and rugged, at the same time as Alanrae and her cousins from the other side. All of them paused, and the king and queen approached the table alone.

Eduardo held forth a scroll and Alanrae took it. She read it over.

"Which one shall be consort?" she asked.

"Michael, the younger," Eduardo replied.

"Johan could not convince you?"

"It is my decision which is most valuable to my house," Eduardo said.

"Michael was well spoken of by the crown prince. A man of courage and loyalty. He will make a noble consort and righteous father. And in compromise, we shall keep the east end of Pious's Fall."

"So let it be written."

Alanrae took a pen from one of the clerics in black leather, wrote upon the scroll, and signed her name. She handed the pen to Eduardo, who signed as well.

"Peace now lays between us," Alanrae said. She looked to Michael and smiled, and Michael saw that she was indeed beautiful. Her eyes lingered on him, searching him, but they seemed at that moment unloving, though certainly powerful.

"May it lay long with the blending of our blood," Eduardo said.

Slowly, they all turned to leave the table, and a great roar went up from both encampments.

Michael took a deep, cleansing breath. The war was at last over.

"What now?" Michael said as they walked back, raising his voice to carry over the sound of shouts and claps, spears on shields, and the sounding of war horns. They entered a vast stretch between the first formations, waving. General Butler stood waiting for them in his full armor, his visor up. He wore a smile that wrinkled his old face beyond its normal hard frown lines.

"We drink and be merry," Eduardo said. "We'll leave three companies on guard at all times, still, for there could still be betrayal or, more likely, misbehavior in the ranks."

"A little tolerance will go a long way toward engendering loyalty at home," Johan said.

"I agree, but this is still an army."

"I meant," Michael said, now having to shout over the cheering. "What is next with Ferralla and Alanrae? When…"

"Details of the marriage will be worked out in due time. You will remain here when we leave, then I or Johan will return as witness for the ceremony. Unless you wish to wed her straight away." Eduardo laughed. "And I would not blame you."

"Luckily, I brought along most of my effects," Michael said. "But I, of course, I would love to-"

Michael stopped suddenly, feeling an odd sensation in his feet.

"What's wrong?" Johan said, stopping and turning back.

"Come along," Eduardo shouted from some paces ahead, not breaking his stride. Butler had fallen in beside him, and they were talking to one another.

"You feel that in the ground? Do you hear that?" Michael said.

"I hear cheering and feel stomping," Johan said.

"There's a…. a whistling."

Johan inclined his head. "I hear that, too."

"No! What I mean is-" Michael broke off as he felt a twig snap in his pocket. "Something's wrong!" He drew his sword. "Father! There's something wrong!"

"What?" Eduardo said, finally pausing. He turned around to face his son, and that is when Michael saw it: a misty smoke was rising from the earth around his father and the general, spreading out over the ground. It seemed to be billowing from the ranks of the soldiers pressed around them as well, but Michael could not see from whence it came.

"Run father!" Michael said, charging up the hill toward the king. He paused in his stride as an arrow landed nearby. He searched around and saw that it had come from their own lines, some twenty yards to his right. A few more arrows were loosed, along with cross-bow bolts, all aimed at him but flying wide of him. "You fools!" Michael shouted. "I'm not trying to kill the king!" Two arrows landed in front of him, and his momentum caused him to fall to avoid them.

He was too late, though. The mist was drawing up, obscuring the king. A curtain of smoke appeared, dashing out into the ranks on either side with supernatural speed. Michael saw rush from the lines, as if sprinting, two indistinct shapes roughly like men. Michael felt the twig in his pocket break two more times. He reached into his jacket and pulled out the bag of charcoal. He flung it as hard as he could toward the king and the general. It burst into a ball of fire and smoke, ash falling in a curtain by the two men.

The two man shapes were clear to see now, covered in burning soot which did not seem to faze them. They were already too close to the king. They seized upon Eduardo, dragging him down to the ground. Black steel flashed in the mist. Butler drew his sword and went to kick one of the shadowy figures, but no sooner had he attacked then both shapes were on him, each wielding a sword and a vicious black dagger. Even in the mist Michael could see the points working into the gaps of Butler's armor as he tumbled. Michael leapt up again, pumping his arms to sprint toward his father. Johan was near him as well, his sword drawn. The lines were holding on either side, uncertain as to what was happening and blinded by the smoke.

As they approached the king, the shapes jumped back. Michael saw two pairs of eyes of shifting colors, glowing with their own inner light, and long, slightly drooping ears above black masks. Their shapes, as Michael watched them regard him, were indistinct around the edges, almost blurry. With a snap of magic, they unleashed a circle of fire that sent Johan diving away. Then they came running toward Michael. He held up his sword, but, as if suddenly aware of the steel, the figures dashed wide.

Michael felt torn for an agonizing moment. He saw his father and Butler lying motionless in front of him, blood oozing from wounds that were barely visible in the ashen smoke. He turned and saw the figures dashing away, smoke and mist encircling them, obscuring their shapes and confusing the lines of fighting men, who were finally moving to attack them.

"Go!" Johan said. "I'll see to Father."

Michael nodded and tore off after the two... *were they elves?* Michael had seen orcs and elves before, but these looked different, their ears, eyes, and hair strange and unfamiliar. He sprinted forward with reckless determination, but the mist that had sprung up during the attack seemed to be following the assassins and thickening, and they were outpacing him easily, becoming mere shadows in a smoky reek. The lines of fighting men shouted from his left, and Michael had to force his watering eyes open to keep sight of his target.

"Here, take my hand!"

Michael had not heard the approach of the galloping horse. On his right appeared Sharona, looking scared, her eyes watering and her face stained with tears. She reached an arm down and Michael grabbed it, nearly pulling her off the horse.

"It's not going to work," Michael said. "Slow down!"

She complied, and he was able to climb on top of the horse and slide down into the saddle behind Sharona. She lashed the reins and Rabble-Rouser took off again, running into the mist.

"I'm sorry," Sharona said. The mist was now swirling all around them, lit only by the dying light of the setting sun in a dull red.

"Just keep on," Michael said. "How can you know where they are in all this?"

"I can feel the magic," Sharona said. "I'm sorry I was too late. I felt them coming."

"Just keep on," Michael said. "I fear they have slain my father."

"They have. Even if he breathes, I fear there will be no healing that can save him. Those daggers have a magic to them."

"Damn it!" Michael said.

They galloped on, until Rabble-Rouser was foaming and crying for a pause, into the mist that led ever onward, the assassins running with inhuman speed, and yet Michael could still catch sight of them in the fog here and there, or at least thought he could. At last, Sharona slowed the beast. Before them rose trees: willows and hemlocks, alongside great oaks, massively tall, tightly grouped, with a diversity of natural paths splitting the foliage, paths which seemed to disappear into glowing obscurity in the mist.

"They're gone," Sharona said.

Michael slid out of the saddle. "They've gone into the wood here."

"Michael!" Sharona said. "Wait, please!"

"There's no time!" Michael said. He stopped, panting, as Sharona cut him off with her horse.

"Michael! Look at the trees."

At last feeling out of breath, Michael looked carefully at the trees, which seemed lit strangely, as if from below, but there was no source to be seen. They, like the assassins, seemed blurry and indistinct, difficult to see clearly. Michael felt almost drunk gazing at them. Above, he could see nothing but mist.

"Where are we?" he said after a moment of wonder. Realization dawned on him. "There's not a forest for miles and miles."

"I don't know," Sharona said. "But those were mages, and dark elves at that. We dare not follow them into that... whatever realm that is, if we even can."

"We have to," Michael said. "They slew my father." He took a deep breath and stepped forward, but even as he did so, the mist seemed to draw back into the wood, and the trees groaned like a great voice. A curtain of red mist obscured their leaves and branches. Michael stopped to watch. He reached to touch a tree trunk, but his hand passed through it. Frightened, he stepped backward, almost falling over. When he approached again, there was only mist over grasses and brush, the image of the trees like colors burned into the eyes from staring at fire.

"What happened?" Michael said.

"I... I only have ideas," Sharona said.

"They're gone. We'll never catch them now," Michael said, staring wide-eyed at where the wood had just been. "Why did you stop us?" he said in a heat of anger, turning back to Sharona.

"I... I said I would protect you, Michael. It's my job to protect you. I'm sorry I couldn't save your father. I was... I was just..." Tears sprang up on her face. "I was just too far away. But *you* are what matters. If you had followed them in there, you would not have returned. The assassins, and the forest too... they were not fully here. We cannot follow them into an echo of their realm without dying. It is like a piece of the Fay, Michael."

Michael nodded slowly, watching the empty space where the wood had been. "Can we follow them at all?"

"Not by those paths, which are made by their magic, but elves, even dark elves, are physical beings and must reside within a tangible realm. Which means it can be reached... somehow."

Michael stood silent for a while, scanning the empty fields that waved in the dying light. He kneeled down and sighed.

"I'm sorry Michael," Sharona said.

"You don't need to be. This wasn't your doing." He shook his head and stood up. "We need to assemble a search team, scour the area. Find out if we can... get wherever they went."

"You will need the mage corps," Sharona said. "Paths between worlds are a tricky business."

Michael sighed. That would mean dealing with Towler, one way or the other.

Sharona and Michael rode with what speed she could still muster from Rabble-Rouser, but the horse was well-winded. They slowed as they approached the great camp, now on high alert with every man armed and already with many soldiers assembling on the field in front of them. It was full night, but Michael could see many torches along the walls of Forgoroto. The gates were not shut, but a great number of fighting men were assembled outside, as if waiting for an attack.

"Exactly what we wished to avoid," Michael said from behind Sharona. "Whoever those assassins were, they want these two armies to kill each other."

"They or whoever hired them," Sharona said. "Dark elves seldom mettle in outside affairs, I am told."

Michael waved to a group of guards outside the pickets, and they parted to let the pair ride into camp. They caught sight of Johan standing outside Towler's tent, along with a gaggle of armed soldiers. Torches lit the avenues of the camp brightly, and the tension was palpable. Michael dismounted and ran forward to his brother. As he approached, Towler emerged from the tent in a device made of polished black steel that held his hands apart and in front of himself, a device he knew was meant to hold against the magic of a mage.

Towler stood defiantly, but swooned slightly, leaning left and right as the soldiers held him up. Morolo, a tall young man with long, black hair who was a lieutenant in the mage corps, stood near at hand, whispering something incoherent to seal or negate the old man's magic.

Johan looked upon him with hard eyes. "I can scarcely wonder why," he said, turning to Michael. "But then, Butler and father are dead… and war looms despite a peace treaty in hand. Who else could have brought such beings into our midsts?"

"So they *are* dead," Michael said. Johan nodded grimly.

"Look to your brat of a brother," Towler said in response, shaking his head as if trying to stay awake. Morolo spoke louder, the syllables in his voice seemingly random.

"The one engaged to a queen and disinherited from the crown? Even if I didn't know assassination to be beyond his character, that is a stretch." Johan scratched his chin.

"I had always assumed he was in league with Ferralla," Michael said. "But this… This is a grim turn for all. Who the hell got to you old man?"

"Nobody," Towler drawled.

Michael felt Sharona wrap her hands around his left arm and squeeze. He caught her worried look.

"Did you search his tent yet?" Michael said.

Johan looked over. "Yes. We found a chest full of beetles that flew away. Some books. Some oddments we ought to look into, and a respectable amount of coin."

"Was there a box of paper?" Michael said desperately. "It was under his secretaire."

"I think he means this, sire," a nearby knight said. He handed to Johan a mangled pile of paper.

Johan handed it to Michael, who visibly collapsed as he sighed. The box was ripped apart, its edges slightly singed as if it had tried to burn.

"We tore it open, but there was just nonsense inside," the knight said.

"There was paper yet inside it?" Michael said. "Where is it?"

The knight handed him a small stack of papers.

"What is this?" Michael said, looking through the stack. "This doesn't look like any language I've heard of." Each page was filled with what looked like a random assortment of letters and punctuation. Even phonetically it was nonsense.

"The wizard's box," Sharona said, taking one of the papers. "It broke the words by rewriting them into nonsense."

"I figured it was some sort of code," Johan said. "I had thought that maybe it could be cracked."

"I don't think so," Sharona said. "This is the work of that box. This is magic."

"Towler's clever," Michael said, looking again to the shifting mage. "Maybe these are in code, but I think Sharona is right. You can look at the format and see that nothing lines up right. We might have lost the only hard evidence we had on him."

"You should have waited for me," Sharona said. "But then, who would know what a paper box meant?"

"Did you catch the assassins?" Johan said.

Michael took a breath. "No. They disappeared into… an enchanted wood."

"They're dark elves," Sharona said. "They fled back into their own realm, probably a memory of when this place was younger."

"How the hell did they get here in the first place?" Michael said.

Morolo spoke up. "They could only be brought forward with the help of magic. You can find such places, I have heard, if you know where the other realm is and you are good at detecting the ley lines of the old creation magic, the places where the prim still washes between the worlds like the sea."

"How strong would a mage have to be to summon those assassins?" Johan said.

Morolo shook his head, holding an eye to Towler as if it was a leash and Towler a defiant dog. "It would have to have been a powerful mage, sire. Very strong and with a mind so expansive as to be able to conceive of two worlds existing simultaneously."

"So only Towler could have done it?" Michael said.

"Or me," Sharona said. Johan paused to look at her, frowning.

"Who is this woman?" Johan said. He squinted and said with sudden realization, "Is that the mage from the battle?"

Michael waved his hands in the air. "Never mind her. She's my… bodyguard. Yes… She's a good battlemage and therefore a good second."

Sharona squinted at Michael and shook her head. "I'm a terrible battle mage. I'm an excellent regular mage, though. I can turn your neck hair into-" Sharona caught the look on Johan's face and stopped short.

"Take Towler to the holding cell," Johan said. "We will need to question him further." He watched the mage being led away, then turned back to Michael. "Do you have any idea who might have put him up to it?"

Michael shook his head. "I thought he was in league with Ferralla… but I don't know anymore. Alanrae wouldn't call battle down upon herself, so soon after a treaty, would she?"

"I doubt it," Johan said. "Severely." His eyes moved from Michael to Sharona. "She would not go to such lengths to lose a husband."

"What if she didn't want to marry Michael?" Sharona said.

"Of course she wanted to," Johan said. "She told me this afternoon she fancied him. Nothing happened that wasn't planned." He looked hard at Michael. "Can I trust you to pursue vengeance with me? Our father was not as gracious to you as he was me."

"Of course," Michael said. "Father was more gracious than you know."

Michael nodded. "Good. I'm reinstating you as captain-errant, now that I'm in command. Assemble your hunting party as you will."

"Aye, sir."

"And make sure your pet mage learns how to address royalty," Johan said, turning away. "You can allow her to be familiar with yourself, but not with me or the peerage."

"Aye," Michael said, and frowned at Sharona.

*

"That was really stupid," Michael said as they walked their horses to the edge of the camp. Michael had gone to retrieve Calot and not spoken to Sharona at all. "Telling my brother it could have been you."

"I didn't say that," Sharona said. "I said only that I could have found the way to summon the men. I couldn't have, though."

"You could or you couldn't?" Michael said.

"I could, but I couldn't. Have." Sharona clenched her fists. "I don't know the area well enough to find the thin spots and move between realms. You saw with that forest how diverse the two locations are."

"Well, could you find those spots?" Michael said.

"Yes," Sharona said. "If you are willing to wait and to allow me to work."

"This is not the kind of time I prefer patience, but if it requires it, I shall have it."

"Good. We'll get started tomorrow."

"Tomorrow?" Michael said. "If you have a way of finding those men, we should be working on it tonight."

"Your father is dead," Sharona said quietly. "Finding them will not bring him or the general back."

"But it *will* bring me peace. I owe revenge for two. Butler is Julia's father, and she will want to see justice done to him."

"I fear your peace is a long way off," Sharona said, her voice soft. "But at the least, I will need sleep tonight. It's essential."

"I suppose you're right," Michael said.

"Of course I'm right. You'll need sleep, too. And time to cry."

"I don't need to cry."

"Yes, you do. You lost your father."

Michael took a breath that hissed between his teeth. "The funeral will be starting soon. Let's fetch Guissali and the others."

"A funeral, already?" Sharona said.

"We are already late on it, considering we are at war again."

***

The massive pyre burned bright and many colored in the night, fed by magic as well as oil. On the highest hilltop it stood, lighting all the grassland about it in flickering green-red, so that it could be espied even from the walls of Forgoroto. Most of the army stood about it, encircling it, watching and waiting. There were more that would prefer to attend, for Eduardo the Black and Butler Dolanari were held in high esteem in the military, but there was still the need for guarding and battle-preparation.

Michael stood on a hillock near at hand, sweating from the heat of the blaze. Sharona was beside him, and he could feel her leaning slightly against him. Guissali and Angelico were also close at hand, but Johan was distant, standing by himself closer to the pyre. Michael's eyes flickered over to Guissali, and he detected eyes that were wet with more than the heat.

"For long years have you served my family," Michael said. Guissali caught his eye and nodded silently. "Be not ashamed of your affections."

DAVID VAN DYKE STEWART

A hush fell over the milling crowd as the high cleric, a white-haired man in loose robes, stepped up near the pyre, a great shadow against its flames. The bodies were brought up on stretchers, covered with white linen, by a group of armored knights. They paused before the fire. An artist a little ways to Michael's left readied himself with his ink set, sitting upon the grass. The catalogue of the king's life was drawing to a close.

"Since when do the people of the divine strand burn their dead?" Sharona said quietly. "I thought you buried them, in the old elven tradition."

"We always have burned men in the field," Michael said.

"Since Pious, my prince," Guissali said. Michael nodded to him. "Since the deeds of Pious we have burned our dead upon the battle-field, that they may not be desecrated by having their bodies reanimated with the echo of their once noble spirits."

"I understand," Sharona said. "I think. It's just a new tradition… or rather, one I did not expect."

"You're new to the army and haven't stood for the end of a battle," Guissali said with a breaking voice. "Confusion is understandable."

The crowd began to murmur again. Michael looked about and saw the men parting to let a group through. It was Alanrae in a dress of black, her face pale and shining brightly in the intense firelight. She was flanked by her cousins, who were unarmed and dressed in equally dark colors. She glanced at Michael as she passed, nodding slightly, then paused near Johan, where she kneeled.

"Peace may not be lost," Angelico said softly. "If we can contain our honor."

"We must," Guissali said.

"I'll see to it," Angelico said, and stepped away, into the crowd.

The high cleric held out his hands from his white robe. Silence returned, and then he spoke, "By the grace of the twelve gods, and by my place as high cleric of the church of the divine, high priest of Artifia, I present the release of two bodies, to honor the return of the souls of two men to the thrones of the gods and the dream eternal. May they find what they sought in life."

With that, the knights threw each of the bodies upon the fire, and flames leapt up high into the sky, bright and eye piercing, fed by the mages who were close by.

"So few words," Sharona said. "The cleric didn't even speak their names."

"This is how it is in war," Michael said. "There are usually too many to name, and here in death we are all equal again."

Despite himself, Michael began to shudder, and fell to his knees. He wept for a man he could not understand. Through his aches he felt Sharona's arms, trying to hold him up, and through his tears, he saw his brother's grim face, and saw the pale face of Alanrae turned to him.

The wracking subsided, and Michael watched as Angelico brought forth a group of knights who surrounded Alanrae, and escorted her through the crowd. As she passed by, she paused for a moment and gazed at Michael, then left.

The crowd began to disperse as the flames fell lower, burning through their fuel and no longer aided by magic.

Michael caught the gaze of Guissali and said, his voice calm again, "We ride early tomorrow, Gui. We have much to do. I want a good group assembled by dawn."

"Aye, sir."

"Yes. We *do* have much to do," Michael said softly.

"I am with you," Sharona.

Michael nodded and walked from the pyre, Sharona following him closely.

END OF BOOK I

ABOUT THE AUTHOR

David Van Dyke Stewart is an author, musician, YouTuber, and educator who currently lives in Modesto, California with his wife and son. He received his musical education as a student of legendary flamenco guitarist Juan Serrano and spent the majority of his 20s as a performer and teacher in California and Nevada before turning his attention to writing fiction, an even older passion than music. He is the author of *Muramasa: Blood Drinker*, a historical fiction novel set in feudal japan, and *Prophet of the Godseed*, a hard-scifi novel that focuses on the consequences of relativity in space travel, as well as numerous novellas, essays, and short stories.

You can find his YouTube channel at http://www.youtube.com/rpmfidel where he creates content on music education (including extensive guitar lessons), literary analysis, movie analysis, philosophy, and logic.

Sign up to his mailing list at http://dvspress.com/list for a free book and advance access to future projects. You can email any questions or concerns to stu@dvspress.com.

Be sure to check http://davidvstewart.com and http://dvspress.com for news and free samples of all his books.

Made in the USA
Columbia, SC
25 November 2019